LITTLE GOLDEN BOOK®

STORY
LAND

40

OF THE BEST
LITTLE
GOLDEN BOOKS
EVER
PUBLISHED

LITTLE GOLDEN BOOK® STORY

LAND

40 OF THE BEST
LITTLE GOLDEN BOOKS
EVER
PUBLISHED

A GOLDEN BOOK · NEW YORK
Western Publishing Company, Inc., Racine, Wisconsin 53404

© 1992, 1991, 1990, 1989, 1988, 1987, 1986, 1985, 1984, 1982, 1981, 1980, 1979, 1978, 1977, 1976, 1975, 1974, 1972, 1970, 1965, 1963, 1962, 1958, 1957, 1956, 1954, 1953, 1952, 1950, 1949, 1948, 1947, 1942 Western Publishing Company, Inc. All rights reserved. Printed in the U.S.A. No part of this book may be reproduced or copied in any form without written permission from the publisher. GOLDEN, GOLDEN & DESIGN, GOLDENCRAFT, and A GOLDEN BOOK are registered trademarks of Western Publishing Company, Inc. Library of Congress Catalog Card Number: 92-70397 ISBN: 0-307-16561-2/ISBN: 0-307-66561-5 (lib. bdg.) MCMXCIV

ACKNOWLEDGMENTS

BIG BIRD BRINGS SPRING TO SESAME STREET: © 1985
Children's Television Workshop. Jim Henson's Sesame Street Muppets
© 1985 Jim Henson Productions, Inc.

BUGS BUNNY STOWAWAY: © 1991 Warner Bros. Inc. LOONEY TUNES
characters, names, and all related indicia are trademarks of Warner Bros. Inc.

THE DAY SNUFFY HAD THE SNIFFLES: © 1988
Children's Television Workshop. Jim Henson's Sesame Street Muppets
© 1988 Jim Henson Productions, Inc.

DONALD DUCK'S CHRISTMAS TREE: © 1991, 1954
The Walt Disney Company.

FIRE ENGINES TO THE RESCUE: Illustrations © 1991 Courtney Studios.

GROVER TAKES CARE OF BABY: © 1987
Children's Television Workshop. Jim Henson's Sesame Street Muppets
© 1987 Jim Henson Productions, Inc.

THE LITTLE MERMAID—ARIEL'S UNDERWATER ADVENTURE:
© 1989 The Walt Disney Company.

MICKEY AND THE BEANSTALK: © 1988 The Walt Disney Company.

MY LITTLE GOLDEN BOOK OF CARS AND TRUCKS: Illustrations
© 1990 Richard and Trish Courtney.

THE NUTCRACKER: Illustrations © 1991 Barbara Lanza.

101 DALMATIANS: © 1991, 1988 The Walt Disney Company. Based on
THE ONE HUNDRED AND ONE DALMATIANS by Dodie Smith,
published by the Viking Press, Inc., copyright 1956 by Dodie Smith.

THE OWL AND THE PUSSYCAT: Illustrations © 1982 Ruth Sanderson.

THE PIED PIPER: Illustrations © 1991 Richard Walz.

PUSS IN BOOTS: Illustrations © 1990, 1986 Lucinda McQueen.

RAPUNZEL: © 1991 Marianna Mayer. Illustrations © 1991 Sheilah Beckett.

TINY DINOSAURS: © 1988 Steven Lindblom. Illustrations © 1988
Gino D'Achille.

TWEETY PLAYS CATCH THE PUDDY TAT: © 1975 Warner Bros. Inc.
LOONEY TUNES characters, names, and all related indicia are trademarks
of Warner Bros. Inc.

THE VELVETEEN RABBIT: Illustrations © 1992 Judith Sutton.

WHAT'S UP IN THE ATTIC?: © 1987 Children's Television Workshop.
Jim Henson's Sesame Street Muppets © 1987 Jim Henson Productions, Inc.

CONTENTS

INTRODUCTION

Little Golden Books, the wonderfully inexpensive picture books with the famous gold-foil bindings, are as familiar to American children as peanut butter and jelly sandwiches. The amazingly popular line, which has now celebrated its fiftieth anniversary, is one of publishing's most remarkable success stories.

How did the Little Golden Books story begin? In the early 1940s there was a small editorial team in New York that called itself the Artists and Writers Guild. The Guild was a branch of Western Printing and Lithographing Company. It was wartime. Toys were scarce. Children's books were expensive, averaging $3.00 for a hardcover title. The Artists and Writers Guild, with the talented George Duplaix and Lucille Ogle at the head, teamed up with Simon & Schuster Publishers and developed an appealing line of hardcover picture books that would cost only 25 cents each. It was a daring plan. To make the line profitable, 50,000 copies of each of the first twelve books had to be printed.

The first titles were conservative choices, concentrating on familiar subjects and stories, such as the Three Little Kittens, a Mother Goose collection, and a book of ABCs. Number "eight" was an exception. It was an original story that happened to "walk in the door," as the editors described it. The title of that risky story was *The Poky Little Puppy*.

The original twelve had the same sturdy board covers that Little Golden Books have today. However, each book also had a blue cloth binding and a colorful dust jacket, both of which were abandoned once the unique gold-foil bindings were used on the books.

The first Little Golden Books were shipped in the fall of 1942. Within days it was clear that the books were selling well. Within months there were two urgent reprint orders. By the end of the first year, close to 2 million copies of Little Golden Books had been sold.

The Poky Little Puppy was a great favorite from the start. After the first list of books, the editors introduced a menagerie of friendly animals to keep Poky company: the Shy Little Kitten, the Saggy Baggy Elephant, and Tawny Scrawny Lion.

For the second list of books, a new category was added, called "here and now stories." The stories were fiction but firmly based on fact. The first of these were *Tootle* and *Scuffy the Tugboat*. Others, like *The Taxi That Hurried* and *Seven Little Postmen*, soon followed. Young readers loved the rhythm and fun in the books and absorbed a good deal of information at the same time.

Through the years many more small books of facts—on machines, the seashore, dogs and cats, dinosaurs, outer space, and many other subjects—continued to round out the line. At one time there was even a small sixteen-volume Little Golden Book Encyclopedia.

The talented list of authors and illustrators who worked on Little Golden Books over the years included such distinguished names as Margaret Wise Brown, Garth Williams, Feodor Rojankovsky, Tibor Gergely, Gustaf Tenggren, Eloise Wilkin, Richard Scarry, Martin and Alice Provensen, Joe Kaufman, Joan Walsh Anglund, J. P. Miller, and many others.

After the start it wasn't long before cartoon and animated characters from movies found their way into the books. Walt Disney titles were published as early as 1944. Bugs Bunny and other Warner Brothers characters joined the line in 1949.

When Little Golden Books began, there was no such thing as television. With the arrival of that "new" invention, popular characters from TV shows joined the line, such as Howdy Doody, Captain Kangaroo, and Lassie. In 1971 the rollicking cast of *Sesame Street* began bringing happy times and easy-to-absorb information to Little Golden Books.

Eventually Western Publishing Company became the exclusive publishers of Little Golden Books. From the early days up to the present, the same wonderful mix of new characters, fact and fancy, fairy tales, and sugar-and-spice-coated lessons has continued in the books. The list has grown. There have been over 1,000 individual titles published—and there is no end in sight.

In fifty years, well over 1 billion Little Golden Books have been printed. To celebrate this Golden Anniversary, we have brought together favorite titles, both old and new. Whether you are reading the stories for the first time or remember them as childhood treasures, we hope they will provide pleasure for today and golden memories for the future.

The Editors

My First Counting Book

By Lilian Moore
Illustrated by Garth Williams

One little puppy,
A roly-poly puppy, alone
as he can be.
"Isn't there a boy or girl
Who wants to play with me?"

Two little woolly lambs
Looking for their mother.
Two little woolly lambs,
A sister and a brother.

Mother Horse
And Daddy Horse
Are proud as they can be . . .

Because they have a baby
    horse,
And Baby Horse makes three.

Four furry, purry kittens
Look alike because

Each furry, purry kitten
Has four white paws.

5

Bunny finds five cabbages—
One, two, three, four, five—

Near the garden wall.
Bunny sniffs five cabbages,
And Bunny wants them all.

One, two, three,
Four, five, six.

First they were eggs . . .
Now they are chicks!

10

Waddle, waddle, waddle,
The baby ducklings go,
Waddling after Mother Duck,
Seven in a row.

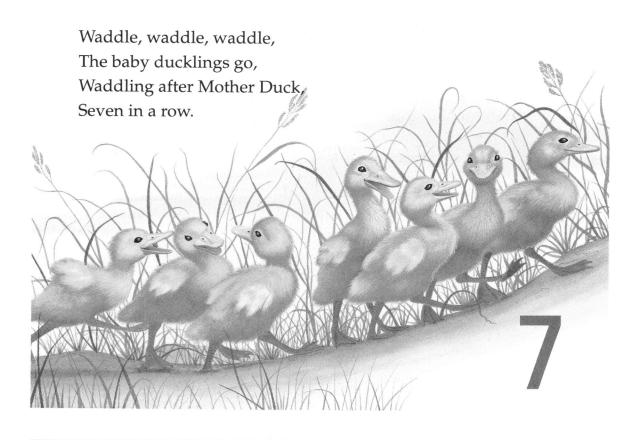

7

Swish, swish,
Eight fish
Swimming in the brook . . .

Swish, swish,
Wise fish,
Swimming past the hook.

8

Hurry and count them
As they fly.

You will see nine geese,
And so will I!

How many nuts did you find,
Little Squirrel,
Looking high and low?
Chitter, chatter,
What's the matter?
Don't you know?

Little Squirrel, I'll tell you,
    then.
Little Squirrel, you found ten.

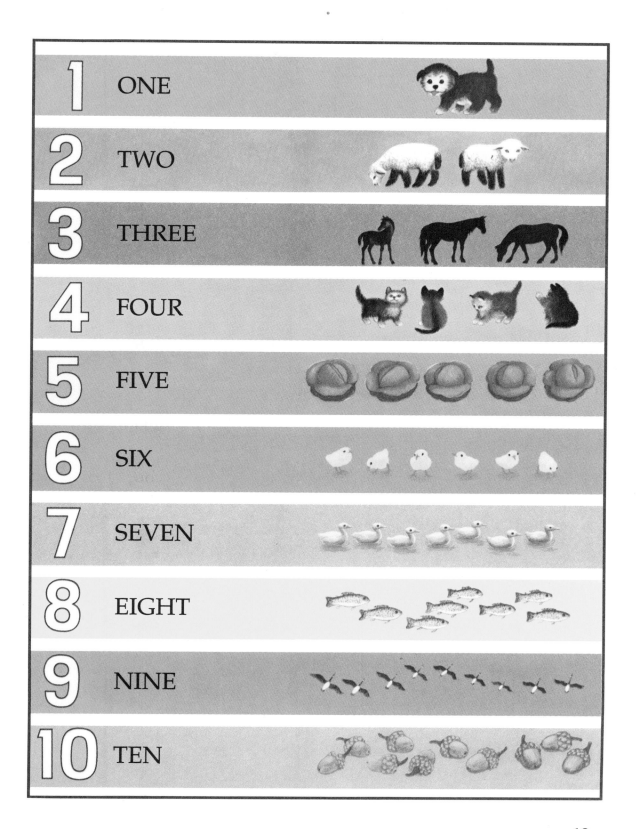

1 ONE

2 TWO

3 THREE

4 FOUR

5 FIVE

6 SIX

7 SEVEN

8 EIGHT

9 NINE

10 TEN

The Three Bears

A Traditional Nursery Tale
Illustrated by Feodor Rojankovsky

Once upon a time there were three bears—a great big papa bear, a middle-sized mama bear, and a wee little baby bear.

They lived in a little house in the forest.

And they had three chairs—a great big chair for the papa bear, a middle-sized chair for the mama bear, and a wee little chair for the baby bear.

And upstairs there were three beds—a great big bed for the papa bear, a middle-sized bed for the mama bear, and a wee little bed for the baby bear.

One morning the mama bear made porridge for breakfast.

She filled a great big bowl for the papa bear, a middle-sized bowl for the mama bear, and a wee little bowl for the baby bear.

But the porridge was too hot to eat, so the three bears went out for a walk in the forest.

15

That same morning a little girl called Goldilocks was walking through the woods.

She came to the three bears' house. And she knocked on the door, but nobody called, "Come in." So she opened the door and went in.

Goldilocks saw the three chairs. She sat in the great big chair. It was too hard. The middle-sized chair was too soft. The baby chair was just right—but it broke when she sat on it.

Now Goldilocks spied the porridge.
"I am hungry," she said.
So she tasted the porridge.
The porridge in the big bowl was too hot.

The porridge in the middle-sized bowl was too cold. The porridge in the wee little bowl was just right—so she ate it all up.

Then Goldilocks went upstairs and tried the beds.

The great big bed was too hard.

The middle-sized bed was too soft.

But the wee little bed was oh, so nice! So Goldilocks lay down and went to sleep.

Then home through the forest and back to their house came the three bears—the great big bear, the middle-sized bear, and the wee little baby bear.

The moment they stepped into the house, they saw that someone had been there.

"Humph!" said the papa bear in his great big voice. "Someone has been sitting in my chair!"

"Land sakes!" said the mama bear in her middle-sized voice. "Someone has been sitting in *my* chair."

"Oh, dear!" cried the baby bear in his wee little voice. "Someone has been sitting in *my* chair, and has broken it all to bits."

Then they all looked at the table.

"Humph," said the papa bear in his great big voice. "Someone has been tasting my porridge."

"And someone has been tasting *my* porridge," said the mama bear.

"Someone has eaten *my* porridge all up," said the baby bear sadly.

Then up the stairs went the three bears, with a thump thump thump, and a trot trot trot, and a skippity-skip-skip. (That was the wee little tiny bear.)

"Humph," said the papa bear in his great big voice.
"Someone has been sleeping in my bed!"

"And someone has been sleeping in *my* bed," said the mama
bear.

"Oh, dear!" cried the baby bear in his wee little voice. "And
someone has been sleeping in *my* bed, and here she is right now!"

Goldilocks opened her eyes and she saw the three bears.

"Oh!" said Goldilocks.

She was so surprised that she jumped right out of the window and she ran all the way home. And she never saw the house in the forest again.

The Poky Little Puppy

By Janette Sebring Lowrey
Illustrated by Gustaf Tenggren

Five little puppies dug a hole under the fence and went for a walk in the wide, wide world.

Through the meadow they went, down the road, over the bridge, across the green grass, and up the hill, one after the other.

22

And when they got to the top of the hill, they counted themselves: one, two, three, four. One little puppy wasn't there.

"Now where in the world is that poky little puppy?" they wondered. For he certainly wasn't on top of the hill.

He wasn't going down the other side. The only thing they could see going down was a fuzzy caterpillar.

He wasn't coming up this side. The only thing they could see coming up was a quick green lizard.

But when they looked down at the grassy place near the bottom of the hill, there he was, running round and round, his nose to the ground.

23

"What is he doing?" the four little puppies asked one another. And down they went to see, roly-poly, pell-mell, tumble-bumble, till they came to the green grass; and there they stopped short.

"What in the world are you doing?" they asked.

"I smell something!" said the poky little puppy.

Then the four little puppies began to sniff, and they smelled it, too.

"Rice pudding!" they said.

And home they went, as fast as they could go, over the bridge, up the road, through the meadow, and under the fence. And there, sure enough, was dinner waiting for them, with rice pudding for dessert.

But their mother was greatly displeased. "So you're the little puppies who dig holes under fences!" she said. "No rice pudding tonight!" And she made them go straight to bed.

But the poky little puppy came home after everyone was sound asleep.

He ate up the rice pudding and crawled into bed as happy as a lark.

The next morning someone had filled the hole and put up a sign. The sign said:

BUT . . .

The five little puppies dug a hole under the fence, just the same, and went for a walk in the wide, wide world.

Through the meadow they went, down the road, over the bridge, across the green grass, and up the hill, two and two. And when they got to the top of the hill, they counted themselves: one, two, three, four. One little puppy wasn't there.

"Now where in the world is that poky little puppy?" they wondered. For he certainly wasn't on top of the hill.

He wasn't going down the other side. The only thing they could see going down was a big black spider.

He wasn't coming up this side. The only thing they could see coming up was a brown hoptoad.

But when they looked down at the grassy place near the bottom of the hill, there was the poky little puppy, sitting still as a stone, with his head on one side and his ears cocked up.

"What is he doing?" the four little puppies asked one another. And down they went to see, roly-poly, pell-mell, tumble-bumble, till they came to the green grass; and there they stopped short.

"What in the world are you doing?" they asked.

"I hear something!" said the poky little puppy.

The four little puppies listened, and they could hear it, too. "Chocolate custard!" they cried. "Someone is spooning it into our bowls!"

And home they went, as fast as they could go, over the bridge, up the road, through the meadow, and under the fence. And there, sure enough, was dinner waiting for them, with chocolate custard for dessert.

26

But their mother was greatly displeased. "So you're the little puppies who will dig holes under fences!" she said. "No chocolate custard tonight!" And she made them go straight to bed.

But the poky little puppy came home after everyone else was sound asleep, and he ate up all the chocolate custard and crawled into bed as happy as a lark.

The next morning someone had filled the hole and put up a sign. The sign said:

DON'T EVER **EVER** DIG HOLES UNDER THIS FENCE!

BUT . . .

In spite of that, the five little puppies dug a hole under the fence and went for a walk in the wide, wide world.

Through the meadow they went, down the road, over the bridge, across the green grass, and up the hill, two and two. And when they got to the top of the hill, they counted themselves: one, two, three, four. One little puppy wasn't there.

"Now where in the world is that poky little puppy?" they wondered. For he certainly wasn't on top of the hill.

He wasn't going down the other side. The only thing they could see going down was a little grass snake.

He wasn't coming up this side. The only thing they could see coming up was a big grasshopper.

But when they looked down at the grassy place near the bottom of the hill, there he was, looking hard at something on the ground in front of him.

"What is he doing?" the four little puppies asked one another. And down they went to see, roly-poly, pell-mell, tumble-bumble, till they came to the green grass; and there they stopped short.

"What in the world are you doing?" they asked.

"I see something!" said the poky little puppy.

The four little puppies looked, and they could see it, too. It was a ripe red strawberry growing there in the grass.

"Strawberry shortcake!" they cried.

And home they went, as fast as they could go, over the bridge, up the road, through the meadow, and under the fence. And there, sure enough, was dinner waiting for them, with strawberry shortcake for dessert.

But their mother said: "So you're the little puppies who dug that hole under the fence again! No strawberry shortcake for supper tonight!" And she made them go straight to bed.

But the four little puppies waited till they thought she was asleep, and then they slipped out and filled up the hole, and when they turned around, there was their mother watching them.

"What good little puppies!" she said. "Come have some strawberry shortcake!"

And this time, when the poky little puppy got home, he had to squeeze in through a wide place in the fence. And there were his four brothers and sisters, licking the last crumbs from their saucer.

"Dear me!" said his mother. "What a pity you're so poky! Now the strawberry shortcake is all gone!"

So poky little puppy had to go to bed without a single bite of shortcake, and he felt very sorry for himself.

And the next morning someone had put up a sign that read:

NO DESSERTS EVER UNLESS PUPPIES NEVER DIG HOLES UNDER THIS FENCE AGAIN!

The Happy Man and His Dump Truck

By Miryam
Illustrated by Tibor Gergely

Once upon a time there was a man who had a dump truck.

Every time he saw a friend, he would wave his hand and tip the dumper.

One day he was riding in his dump truck, singing a happy song, when he met a pig going along the road.

31

"Would you like a ride in my dump truck?" he asked.

"Oh, thank you!" said the pig. And he climbed into the back of the truck.

After they had gone a little way down the road, the man saw a friend.

He waved his hand and tipped the dumper.

"Whee," said the pig. "What fun!" And he slid all the way down to the bottom of the dumper.

Very soon they came to a farm.

32

"Here is where my friends live," said the pig. "You have a nice dump truck.

"Would you please let my friends see your truck?"

"I will give them a ride in my dump truck," said the man.

So the hen and the rooster climbed into the truck.

And the duck climbed into the truck.

And the dog and the cat climbed into the truck.

And the pig climbed back into the truck, too.

And the man closed the tailgate so they would not fall out.

And then off they went!

They went past the farm, and all the animals waved to the farmer.

The man was very happy. "They are all my friends," he said.

So he waved his hand and tipped the dumper.

The hen, the rooster, the duck, the dog, the cat, and the pig all slid down the dumper into a big heap!

The animals were all so happy!

Then the man took them for a long ride, and drove them back to the farm.

He opened the tailgate wide and raised the dumper all the way up.

All the animals slid off the truck onto the ground.

"What a fine sliding board," they all said.

"Thank you," said all the animals.

"Cut, cut," clucked the hen.

"Cock-a-doodle-doo," the rooster crowed.

"Quack, quack," quacked the duck.

"Bow-wow," barked the dog.

"Meow, meow," mewed the cat.

And the pig said a great big grunt. "Oink, oink!"

The man waved his hand and tipped the dumper, and he rode off in his dump truck, singing a happy song.

The Little Red Hen

A Traditional Nursery Tale
Illustrated by J. P. Miller

One summer day the little Red Hen found a grain of wheat.

"A grain of wheat!" said the little Red Hen to herself. "I will plant it."

She asked the duck:

"Will you help me plant this grain of wheat?"

"Not I!" said the duck.

She asked the goose:

"Will you help me plant this grain of wheat?"

"Not I!" said the goose.

She asked the cat:

"Will you help me plant this grain of wheat?"

"Not I!" said the cat.

She asked the pig:

"Will you help me plant this grain of wheat?"

"Not I!" said the pig.

"Then I will plant it myself," said the little Red Hen. And she did.

Soon the wheat grew tall, and the little Red Hen knew it was time to reap it.

"Who will help me reap the wheat?" she asked.

"Not I!" said the duck.

"Not I!" said the goose.

"Not I!" said the cat.

"Not I!" said the pig.

"Then I will reap it myself," said the little Red Hen. And she did.

She reaped the wheat, and it was ready to be taken to the mill and made into flour.

"Who will help me carry the wheat to the mill?" she asked.

"Not I!" said the duck.

"Not I!" said the goose.

"Not I!" said the cat.

"Not I!" said the pig.

"Then I will carry it myself," said the little Red Hen. And she did. She carried the wheat to the mill, and the miller made it into flour.

When she got home, she asked, "Who will help me make the flour into dough?"

"Not I!" said the duck.

"Not I!" said the goose.

"Not I!" said the cat.

"Not I!" said the pig.

"Then I will make the dough myself," said the little Red Hen. And she did.

Soon the bread was ready to go into the oven.

"Who will help me bake this bread?" said the little Red Hen.

"Not I!" said the duck.

"Not I!" said the goose.

"Not I!" said the cat.

"Not I!" said the pig.

"Then I will bake it myself," said the little Red Hen. And she did.

After the loaf had been taken from the oven, it was set on the windowsill to cool.

"And now," said the little Red Hen, "who will help me to eat the bread?"

"I will!" said the duck.

"I will!" said the goose.

"I will!" said the cat.

"I will!" said the pig.

"No, I will eat it myself!" said the little Red Hen. And she did.

The Color Kittens

By Margaret Wise Brown
Illustrated by Alice and Martin Provensen

Once there were two color kittens with green eyes, Brush and Hush. They liked to mix and make colors by splashing one color into another. They had buckets and buckets and buckets and buckets of color to splash around with. Out of these colors they would make all the colors in the world.

The buckets had the colors written on them, but, of course, the kittens couldn't read. They had to tell by the colors. "It is very easy," said Brush.

"Red is red. Blue is blue," said Hush.

But they had no green. "No green paint!" said Brush and Hush. And they wanted green paint, of course, because nearly every place they liked to go was green.

Green as cats' eyes
Green as grass
By streams of water
Green as glass.

So they tried to make some
green paint.

Brush mixed red paint and
white paint together—and what
did that make? It didn't make green.
But it made pink.

Pink as pigs
Pink as toes
Pink as a rose
Or a baby's nose.

Then Hush mixed yellow and
red together, and it made orange.

Orange as an orange tree
Orange as a bumblebee
Orange as the setting sun
Sinking slowly in the sea.

The kittens were delighted, but
it didn't make green.

Then they mixed red and blue together—and what did that make? It didn't make green. It made a deep dark purple.

Purple as violets
Purple as plums
Purple as shadows
On late afternoons.

Still no green! And then . . .

O wonderful kittens! O Brush! O Hush!

At last, almost by accident, the kittens poured a bucket of blue and a bucket of yellow together, and it came to pass that they made a green as green as grass.

Green as green leaves on a tree
Green as islands in the sea.

The little kittens were so happy with all the colors they had made that they began to paint everything around them. They painted . . .

Green leaves
    and red berries
    and purple flowers
    and pink cherries
Red tables
    and yellow chairs
Black trees
    with golden pears.

Then the kittens got so excited, they knocked their buckets upside down and all the colors ran together. Yellow, red, a little blue, and a little black . . . and that made brown.

Brown as a tugboat
Brown as an old goat
Brown as a beaver.

And in all that brown, the sun went down. It was evening and the colors began to disappear in the warm dark night.

The kittens fell asleep in the warm dark night with all their
colors out of sight, and as they slept they dreamed their dream—

A wonderful dream
Of a red rose tree
That turned all white
When you counted three

One . . . TWO . . . **THREE**

Of a purple land
In a pale pink sea

Where apples fell
From a golden tree

And then a world of Easter eggs
That danced about on little short legs.

And they dreamed that
A green cat danced
With a little pink dog
Till they all disappeared
    in a soft gray fog.

And suddenly Brush woke up and Hush woke up. It was morning. They crawled out of bed into a big bright world. The sky was wild with sunshine.

The kittens were wild with purring and pouncing—

Pounce

Pounce

Pounce

They got so pouncy, they knocked over the buckets and all the colors ran out together.

There were all the colors in the world and the color kittens had made them.

The Little Red Caboose

By Marian Potter
Illustrated by Tibor Gergely

The little red caboose always came last.

First came the big black engine, puffing and chuffing.

Then came the boxcars, then the oil cars, then the coal cars, then the flatcars. Sometimes they were switched around in different ways. But the little red caboose always came last.

49

Boys and girls waved at the big black engine. They listened to the boxcars and the oil cars and the coal cars and the flatcars go *clickety-clack*.

But by the time the little red caboose came along, the boys and girls were turning away.

Because the little red caboose always came last.

"Oh, smoke!" said the little red caboose. "I wish
I were a flatcar or a coal car or an oil car or a boxcar,
so boys and girls would wave at me.

"How I wish I were a big black engine, puffing
and chuffing way up at the front of the train!

"But I'm just the little old red caboose.
Nobody cares for me."

One day the train started up a mountain.

Up went the big black engine.

Up went the boxcars.

Up went the oil cars.

Up went the coal cars.

Up went the flatcars.

Up went the little red caboose.

"Hang on tight, little caboose," called the flatcar. "This is a long tall mountain. And you are the last car on the train."

"Don't I know it!" said the little red caboose with a sigh. "Poor me!"

The train went slower and slower and s-l-o-w-e-r.

It looked as if that train could not get up the mountain.

"Look out, little caboose!" called the flatcar. "The train is starting to slip back down this long tall mountain!"

"Not if I can help it!" said the little red caboose.

And he slammed on his brakes.

And he held tight to the tracks.

And he kept that train from sliding down the mountain!

Then—*bump!*

The little red caboose felt something push him from behind. It was two big black engines. They pushed the train up to the top of the mountain.

"We couldn't have done it," said the big black engines, "if it had not been for the little red caboose."

Everyone cheered. And the little red caboose nearly burst with pride.

Now children wave at the big black engine and at all the cars.

But they save their biggest waves for the little red caboose. Because the little red caboose saved the train.

Grover
Takes Care of Baby

By Emily Thompson
Illustrated by Tom Cooke

While walking home from the playground one day, Grover dropped his ball, and it rolled right under a baby carriage.

"Please excuse me," said Grover. "Oh, hello, Marsha! Who is this?"

"Hi, Grover," said Marsha. "This is Max, my baby brother. I'm taking care of him while Mommy and Daddy are at work."

"Oh, he is cute and adorable!" said Grover. "What do you do with him?"

"I play with him, take him for walks, help feed him, give him his baths, and put him to bed," said Marsha.

"I would like to take care of a baby, too," said Grover. "I have a new baby cousin named Emily. I, lovable, helpful old Grover, would take good care of the baby Emily."

Grover waved good-bye to Marsha and Max.

I would let her play with my toys. I would show Emily how to climb mountains . . . go through tunnels . . . and leap tall buildings in a single bound!

If Baby Emily came for a visit, I would help her get dressed.

I would introduce Emily to all my friends at play group. Oh, I would be so proud!

But what if she tore my picture? Oh, I would be so embarrassed!

Mrs. Brown would say, "Never mind, Grover, we can fix it."

After play group, we could go shopping . . . and for a walk.

We could do our exercises together. One and two and—pant, pant!—three. Now touch those toes!

We could play peekaboo . . . and eensy-weensy spider.

At dinnertime I would help my mommy feed Emily in her high chair. I would tie on her bib, and make sure her milk wasn't too hot, and cut up her carrots, and wipe up her dribbles.

"Emily, sweetie, you need a bath. You are a mess!"

At bathtime I would be ready. I would pour in the bubbles . . . and test the temperature. Then I would duck.

At bedtime I would help Emily listen to a story.

Then I would sing her a lullaby, kiss her nose, and turn on the night-light. I would even let her borrow my teddy monster to cuddle.

I, Grover, would be a big help.

56

"Oh, Grover, I am so glad you are home," said Grover's mommy as she opened the door of their apartment. "Guess what! Aunt Betsy and Uncle Ralph are bringing your baby cousin, Emily, for a visit. How would you like to help take care of the baby?

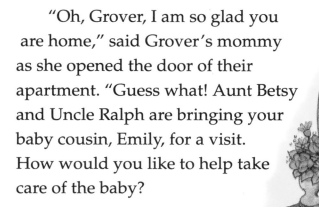

"Grover, you are very good at taking care of baby monster!" said his mommy.

The Jolly Barnyard

By Annie North Bedford
Illustrated by Tibor Gergely

Said Farmer Brown, "Tra-la, tra-lee!
Today is my birthday, lucky me!
I'll give my animals all a treat—
They'll get what they like best to eat."

He took a pan of oats, of course,
To the baby colt and the mother horse.
For the cow and the calf he set corn down,
"Cause today is my birthday," said Farmer Brown.

The big white ram and the fat black sheep
Got lots of grain in a great big heap.
The gobbling turkey kept eating until
He had to admit he'd eaten his fill.

The chickens and rooster ate all their food;
There was more than enough for their hungry brood.
The duck ate her food, and so did the drake,
And so did their ducklings down by the lake.

The dog got bones to bury and chew.
The cat got milk, and her kitten did, too.

When all the animals had been fed,
Farmer Brown left, and the spotted cow said:
"Kind Farmer Brown! Wouldn't you say
We should give him a treat for his birthday?"

"Neigh! We'll pull his wagon without a jolt,"
Said the big brown horse and her little brown colt.
"Moo-oo!" said the cow. "I'll give him milk to drink."
Said her calf, "So will I, someday, I think!"

"Baa-aa! We'll give him fine wool," said the sheep,
"For our fleece is soft and warm and deep."
"Gobble!" said the turkey. "On Thanksgiving Day,
I'll dress up his table in my own special way."

"Cluck!" said the hen. "I'll give eggs fresh and white."
Said the rooster, "I'll wake him as soon as it's light."
"Quack!" said the duck and the drake. "Farmer Brown
Can make cozy pillows with our fluffy down."

"Bow-wow!" said the dog. "When the Farmer's away,
I'll watch over his house both night and day."
"Meow!" said the cat. "My brave kitten and I
Will catch all the mice—not a one will get by!"

Inside the farmhouse was one more fine treat—
A beautiful cake for the Farmer to eat.

Happy Birthday, Farmer Brown!

Chipmunk's ABC

By Roberta Miller
Illustrated by Richard Scarry

A is for **apple tree**.

B is for **burrow**. Guess who lives in the **burrow** under the apple tree.

C is for **Chipmunk**. It is **Chipmunk** who lives in the burrow under the apple tree.

D is for **Donkey**. Chipmunk and **Donkey** have been out picking **daffodils**.

E is for **ears**. Chipmunk's mother washes his **ears**.

F is for **friends**. Chipmunk has many good **friends**. **Froggie** is a **friend**.

G is for **Goat**. **Goat** plays a **game** with Chipmunk.

H is for **hide-and-seek**.
Chipmunk and his friends **hide** in **holes** and **hedges**.

I is for **ice cream**.
Donkey is serving **ice cream**.

J is for **jump**. Froggie **jumps** for **joy**.
He loves ice cream.

K is for **kitchen**. In the **kitchen**, Chipmunk puts the **kettle** on. Mouse slices cheese with a **knife**.

L is for **lake**. Chipmunk and Bunny go sailing on the **lake**. They wear **life jackets**.

M is for **Mouse**. **Mouse** has the **mumps**. He listens to **music** and has his **meals** in bed.

N is for **net**. Chipmunk catches butterflies in his **net**.

O is for **oboe**. Froggie plays the **oboe**. Donkey drinks from an **orange** cup.

P is for **party**. Chipmunk loves **parties**. Mouse has gotten over the mumps. He has brought Chipmunk a **present**—a bunch of **pansies**.

Q is for **quilt**. Chipmunk's mother is making a **quilt**.

R is for **river**, where Chipmunk and Donkey are having a swimming **race**.

68

S is for **swing**. Chipmunk likes to **swing** almost as much as he likes to **swim**.

T is for **telephone**. Someone wants to **talk** to Chipmunk.

U is for **umbrella** to shade Chipmunk's mother from the sun.

V is for **vacation**. Chipmunk and his mother are at the seashore, staying in a **villa** with a nice **view** of the sea.

W is for **wagon**. Goat pulls the **wagon** and Chipmunk rides. The **weather** is nice, and they have a **watermelon** to eat.

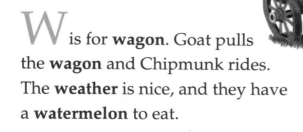

X is a letter. Chipmunk and Bunny play tic-tac-toe with an **X** and an O.

Y is for **yellow**. **Yellow** flowers grow in Chipmunk's **yard**.

Z is for **zipper**. Chipmunk **zips** his jacket. He is going outside to play with his friends. Have fun, Chipmunk!

Tweety Plays Catch the Puddy Tat

By Eileen Daly

Illustrated by Peter Alvarado and William Lorencz

I *think I'd better find that puddy tat*, Tweety decided. *He's always twying to catch me, so I'm safer if I know where he is!* He flew down to the floor, hoping to see Sylvester curled up in his favorite snoozing place.

But Sylvester was in the kitchen, and he seemed very busy. Tweety peeked around the corner.

"I wonder what the puddy tat is cooking," said Tweety to himself. "It smells vewy tasty."

Then he heard Sylvester call, "Tweety! Tweety Bird! I've got a present for you."

Oh, goody! thought Tweety. *The puddy tat wants to be fwiends again.* He flew into the kitchen. "What's my pwesent?" he asked.

"Birdseed flapjacks," said Sylvester, "made just for you." He flipped one quickly into the air, and it fell—*plop!*—right on Tweety.

"O-o-oh!" cried Tweety. "My fwapjack is *too big*!"

"Not for me," said Sylvester. "It's just right, with a Tweety Bird inside." He pounced, but the flapjack—and Tweety—disappeared under the stove.

"That was a naughty puddy tat," said Tweety. "I would wike to be fwiends with you, but you make it so hard."

"No harm meant, Tweety," said Sylvester. "I just like to play 'Catch the Tweety Bird.'"

"Let's pway 'Catch the Puddy Tat' for a wittle while," suggested Tweety, but Sylvester just yawned and fell asleep.

Tweety escaped from under the stove and flew up to the attic.

"I weally need a west fwom that puddy tat," he said as he perched on a birdcage. "How can I make him stop chasing me?"

Then Tweety looked into the cage and had an idea. He searched the attic and finally found just what he wanted—a paper bird hanging from a string.

Tweety put the paper bird far back inside the cage. "Puddy Tat will think the bird is a weal one. He will have to go inside to get it—and I will twap him in the birdcage."

Tweety hid beside the open birdcage door. Then he began to sing.

Soon he heard Sylvester call, "Tweety? Did I hear you up here?"

Suddenly Sylvester spied the cage and, inside, what he thought was a bird. "Aha!" he exclaimed and pounced into the open cage.

Tweety slammed the door shut. "Aha yourself!" he said. "Now you can't get out, and I will have a west."

"A rest, eh?" said Sylvester after a minute. "Well, keep your eyes open, Tweety. I think you are about to see a cage walking."

Sylvester put his legs through the wires and walked away to find a wire cutter.

Soon he had cut his way out and was again chasing poor Tweety.

"Puddy Tat," Tweety puffed, out of breath, "I am getting so vewy sweepy. I wish you would go away for a wong time."

Later Tweety asked himself, "What *would* make him go away? Something scawy, maybe . . ."

While Sylvester was sleeping, Tweety thought and thought. *That puddy tat is pwetty bwave*, recalled Tweety. *It will take something* weally *scawy to fwighten him away.*

"I know," he said. "I'll be a witch—a scawy witch. That should make the puddy tat go away for a w-o-o-ong time."

Tweety made himself look like a scary witch. He flew over Sylvester's head. *Swish!*

"*Woooo-oo-OOO!*" said the Tweety-witch.

Sylvester opened one eye. Then he opened the other. "Wh-what was *that*?" he asked, standing up and looking around.

"A witch," said the Tweety-witch.

"A witch, eh?" said Sylvester. "You're a very small witch, aren't you?"

"Well, yes," said the Tweety-witch. "But you know what small witches do, don't you?"

"What?" asked Sylvester, backing away just a little bit.

"We cast spells—*bad* ones. We can change cats into tiny mice."

"Into m-mice! Can you—uh—*really* do that?" asked Sylvester, backing away a little faster.

"It's my favowite spell," said the Tweety-witch. "I'll show you." He began to wave his broom.

"No! Don't!" shouted Sylvester, and he ran out the door and through the gate.

"I'm starting the spell," said the Tweety-witch as he flew just above Sylvester's ear. "One, two, *ka-zip, ka-zip* . . ."

Sylvester ran faster—so fast that he didn't see where he was going.

"Wook out!" shouted Tweety, but it was too late. Sylvester was right at the edge of a pond. He couldn't stop, so he took a mighty leap and landed beside a big rock. After a minute, he

climbed up on the rock. He looked back and saw Tweety,
who had taken off his witch mask.

"Tweety!" exclaimed Sylvester. Then he said, "I—uh—knew
that was you all the time."

"Are you all wight, Puddy Tat?" Tweety called.

"No!" said Sylvester. "Cats don't like water. Help me!"
Sylvester pointed to the shore. "Sail that little boat over and
rescue me."

But Tweety wouldn't do it. "You were a naughty puddy tat,"
he said, and he flew home, leaving Sylvester marooned.

For a little while, Tweety was happy all by himself. Then a strange thing happened. He grew lonesome. "I never thought I'd miss that pesky puddy tat," he said to himself. "I even miss being chased!"

Finally he flew back to see how Sylvester was getting along. And what did Tweety find? Sylvester was even more lonesome than Tweety!

"Poor Puddy Tat," said Tweety. "If I wescue you, will you pwomise not to pway chase *all* the time?"

"I promise, I promise," said Sylvester.

So Tweety sailed the little boat over to the rock, and Sylvester sailed it back.

And the next day Sylvester chased Tweety only twice—once before breakfast and once before dinner.

The Owl
and the Pussycat

By Edward Lear
Illustrated by Ruth Sanderson

The Owl and the Pussycat went to sea
In a beautiful pea-green boat:
They took some honey, and plenty of money
Wrapped up in a five-pound note.

The Owl looked up to the stars above,
    And sang to a small guitar,
"O lovely Pussy, O Pussy, my love,
    What a beautiful Pussy you are,
        You are,
        You are!
    What a beautiful Pussy you are!"

Pussy said to the Owl, "You elegant fowl,
    How charmingly sweet you sing!
Oh! let us be married; too long we have tarried;
    But what shall we do for a ring?"

They sailed away, for a year and a day,
    To the land where the bong-tree grows;
And there in a wood a Piggy-wig stood,
    With a ring at the end of his nose,
        His nose,
        His nose,
    With a ring at the end of his nose.

"Dear Pig, are you willing to sell for one shilling
    Your ring?" Said the Piggy, "I will."
So they took it away, and were married next day
    By the Turkey who lives on the hill.

They dined on mince and slices of quince,
    Which they ate with a runcible spoon;
And hand in hand, on the edge of the sand,
    They danced by the light of the moon,
        The moon,
        The moon,
    They danced by the light of the moon.

The Day Snuffy Had the Sniffles

By Linda Lee Maifair

Illustrated by Tom Brannon

Oscar the Grouch popped up out of his can just in time to see Big Bird skipping down Sesame Street. "Go away, Bird!" Oscar grumbled. "All that cheerfulness will ruin my day. Besides, it's time to collect the trash. I'm too busy to talk to you."

"That's okay, Oscar," Big Bird said. "I'm in a big hurry to get to Snuffy's house so I can cheer him up. He has the sniffles."

"Grouches don't know anything about cheering anybody up," said Oscar, "but we do know a lot about the sniffles. I have just the thing for you to take to old snuffle-nose. Wait here!"

Before Big Bird could say anything, Oscar disappeared into his can, banging the lid shut behind him.

Big Bird was waiting impatiently for Oscar when Cookie Monster came along.

"What's the matter?" Cookie asked Big Bird. "Somebody eat all your cookies?"

"Worse than that," Big Bird said. "Snuffy's got the sniffles and can't come out to play. I'm waiting for Oscar. He has a surprise for me to take to Snuffy."

"Cheer-up surprise?" said Cookie Monster. "Wait here!" He left in such a rush that he nearly ran into Bert.

As soon as Bert heard that Snuffy had the sniffles, he told Big Bird, "I know just the thing to cheer up a sniffly Snuffleupagus. Wait here!" He dashed into 123 Sesame Street before Big Bird could open his beak to say one word.

Big Bird plopped down on the steps next to Oscar's can. "At this rate I'll *never* get to see Snuffy!" he said. He tapped his foot. He stood up. He paced back and forth. He sat down. Then he did the same thing all over again.

Just when Big Bird decided that he couldn't wait one second longer, Bert ran down the steps and handed him a large shoe box. Big Bird peeked inside.

"It's my bottle cap collection," Bert said proudly. "You can lend it to Snuffy. It will give him something fascinating to look at while he's sick in bed. There's nothing more exciting than bottle caps, except maybe paper clips."

Before Big Bird could answer, Cookie Monster came back. Huffing and puffing, he held out a slightly dented cookie tin.

"Gee, thanks, Cookie," Big Bird said. He tugged at the lid. "I just know Snuffy will enjoy all these . . . COOKIE CRUMBS?"

Cookie Monster shrugged. "Well," he said, "it's the thought that counts." He brushed chocolate chips and cookie crumbs off his tummy. "Sure cheered me up!" he said.

Just then Oscar popped back up. "Here, Bird," he said, "the perfect thing for old Sniffy." He placed a jar of something lumpy and green on top of the shoe box and cookie tin.

"It's an old Grouch family recipe, handed down from grand-grouch to momgrouch. It's sure to cure even Snuffleupagus-sized sniffles—sardine-and-sauerkraut soup!" Oscar said.

Bert and Cookie Monster held their noses. "Blecch!" they said.

"You'd better get a move on, Bird," said Oscar. "Can't let that soup get too warm. Sardine-and-sauerkraut soup only tastes its worst when it's good and cold."

Juggling the shoe box, the cookie tin, and the smelly Grouch soup, Big Bird started off again. He was glad to be on his way to Snuffy's at last. He got as far as the library when he met Betty Lou.

As soon as she heard where Big Bird was going, Betty Lou said, "I know just the thing to cheer up Snuffy. Come on!"

Before Big Bird could make a peep, Betty Lou took him up the steps and into the library.

"Everybody's sure in a hurry to make me wait!" said Big Bird, looking around. Finally Betty Lou came back.

84

She balanced a thick book on top of Big Bird's bundles. "Here's an animal picture book for Snuffy to look at all by himself. And here's a monster storybook for his mother to read to him." She piled an even thicker book on top of the first one.

"There's nothing like a good book to cheer you up!" said Betty Lou.

Big Bird's arms were so full, he couldn't wave good-bye to Betty Lou. "It's a good thing Snuffy's cave isn't far!" he said.

"What do you have there, Big Bird?" the Count called from his castle window. "One shoe box! One tin! One jar! Two books! Wonderful!"

Big Bird told the Count why he was in a hurry. "I have just the thing for your friend," the Count said. "Wait there!"

After what seemed like hours to Big Bird, the Count came out of his castle and handed him a box of tissues.

"Snuffy can count them and count them as much as he pleases, and they'll come in handy whenever he sneezes!" the Count said.

Crinkled, wrinkled tissues stuck out of the box.

"I counted them myself. There are two hundred tissues!" the Count said.

Big Bird tiptoed quietly past Gladys's barn.

"My, my, you do have your hands full," said Gladys the cow.

"These are surprises for Snuffy," Big Bird explained. "He has the sniffles. I've been trying all morning to go cheer him up."

"Well, any cow knows there's only one way to do that," Gladys said. "Wait here!"

"Not again!" Big Bird said. But Gladys had already trotted into the barn.

Gladys's cheer-up present turned out to be a pint of ice cream. It was getting soft and soggy in the noontime sun. "Nothing puts you in a good *mooood* like ice cream," Gladys said. Her bell tinkled as she balanced the squishy ice-cream carton on top of the wrinkled tissues and the books and the jar and the empty cookie tin and the shoe box.

Big Bird watched the sticky pink drops fall onto his toes.

"It's strawberry," Gladys explained.

At last Big Bird made it to Snuffy's cave without dropping a single present.

He pushed open the front door with his foot.

Then he had a terrible thought. "I brought all these presents for Snuffy and not a single one of them is from *me*! I forgot to bring Snuffy a present!"

Big Bird sighed a deep sigh and shifted the slippery pile of presents. "I hope Snuffy won't be too disappointed," he said.

And there was Snuffy, propped up on huge stuffed pillows in his Snuffleupagus-sized bed. On a tray in front of him was a glass of orange juice, a box of cough drops, a coloring book, and a box of crayons.

Snuffy had an ice pack on his head and a thermometer sticking out of his mouth.

Mrs. Snuffleupagus took the thermometer out of Snuffy's mouth and studied it for a moment. "No more fever!" she said.

She took a bottle and measured the thick orange sniffles medicine into a spoon. Snuffy swallowed it all.

Mrs. Snuffleupagus gave him a big hug. "Cheer up, son," she told him. "You'll be out of that bed in no time!"

"Uh-oh!" Big Bird said. The cheer-up surprises were slipping from his grasp.

"Ah . . . Ah . . . CHOO!" Snuffy sneezed a gigantic snuffle sneeze that rattled everything in the room. The presents crashed to the floor!

"Oh, dear!" said Mrs. Snuffleupagus.

Big Bird stood in the doorway, feeling sadder than ever. How could he cheer up Snuffy now?

Snuffy blew his snuffle on a handkerchief the size of a tablecloth. Then he smiled at Big Bird. "Oh, Bird," he snuffled, "how did you guess what I wanted to cheer me up?"

Big Bird stared at the mess on the floor. "What's that, Snuffy?" he asked. "The bottle caps? The cookie crumbs? The melted ice cream? Or the sardine-and-sauerkraut soup?"

"No, Bird," said Snuffy, "a visit from *you*!"

That cheered up Big Bird, too!

My Little Golden Book About God

By Jane Werner Watson
Illustrated by Eloise Wilkin

GOD IS GREAT.

Look at the stars in the evening sky,
so many millions of miles away
that the light you see shining left its star
long, long years before you were born.
Yet even beyond the farthest star,
God knows the way.

89

Think of the snowcapped mountain peaks.
Those peaks were crumbling away with age
before the first men lived on earth.
Yet when they were raised up sharp and new,
God was there, too.

Bend down to touch the smallest flower.
Watch the busy ant tugging at his load.
See the flash of jewels on the insect's back.
This tiny world your two hands could span,
like the oceans and mountains and far-off stars,
God planned.

Think of our earth, spinning in space,
so that now, for a day of play and work,
we face the sunlight, then we turn away—
to the still, soft darkness for rest and sleep.
This, too, is God's doing.
For GOD IS GOOD.

God gives us everything we need—
shelter from cold and wind and rain,
clothes to wear, and food to eat.
God gives us flowers, the songs of birds,
the laughter of brooks, the deep song of the sea.

He sends the sunshine to make things grow,
sends in its turn the needed rain.
God makes us grow, too, with minds and eyes
to look about our wonderful world,
to see its beauty, to feel its might.
He gives us a small, still voice in our hearts
to help us tell wrong from right.
God gives us hopes and wishes and dreams,
plans for our grown-up years ahead.
He gives us memories of yesterdays,

so that happy times and people we love
we can keep with us always in our hearts.
For GOD IS LOVE.

God is the love of our mother's kiss,
the warm, strong hug of our daddy's arms.
God is in all the love we feel
for playmates and family and friends.
When we're hurt or sorry or lonely or sad,
if we think of God, He is with us there.

God whispers to us in our hearts:

"Do not fear, I am here
And I love you, my dear.
Close your eyes and sleep tight
For tomorrow will be bright—
All is well, dear child.
Good night."

The Tale of Peter Rabbit

By Beatrix Potter
Illustrated by Adriana Mazza Saviozzi

Once upon a time there were four little Rabbits, and their names were—Flopsy, Mopsy, Cotton-tail, and Peter. They lived with their mother in a sandbank, underneath the root of a very big fir tree.

"Now, my dears," said old Mrs. Rabbit one morning, "you may go into the fields or down the lane, but don't go into Mr. McGregor's garden. Your father had an accident there—he was put in a pie by Mrs. McGregor. Now run along and don't get into mischief. I am going out."

Then old Mrs. Rabbit took a basket and her umbrella, and went through the wood to the baker's. She bought a loaf of brown bread and five currant buns.

Flopsy, Mopsy, and Cotton-tail, who were good little bunnies, went down the lane to gather blackberries. But Peter, who was very naughty, ran straight away to Mr. McGregor's garden and squeezed under the gate!

First he ate some lettuces and some French beans, and then he ate some radishes. And then, feeling rather sick, he went to look for some parsley.

But round the end of a cucumber frame, whom should he meet but Mr. McGregor! Mr. McGregor was on his hands and knees planting out young cabbages, but he jumped up and ran after Peter, waving a rake and calling out, "Stop, thief!"

Peter was most dreadfully frightened. He rushed all over the garden, for he had forgotten the way back to the gate.

He lost one of his shoes among the cabbages, and the other shoe amongst the potatoes. After losing them he ran on four legs and went faster, so that he might have got away altogether if . . . he had not unfortunately run into a gooseberry net, and got caught by the large buttons on his jacket. It was a blue jacket with brass buttons, quite new.

Peter gave himself up for lost, and shed big tears. But his sobs were overheard by some friendly sparrows, who flew to him in great excitement, and implored him to exert himself.

Mr. McGregor came up with a sieve, which he intended to pop upon the top of Peter. But Peter wriggled out just in time, leaving his jacket behind, and rushed into the tool shed, and jumped into a can. It would have been a beautiful thing to hide in, if it had not had so much water in it.

Mr. McGregor was quite sure that Peter was somewhere in the tool shed, perhaps hidden underneath a flowerpot. He began to turn them over carefully, looking under each.

Presently Peter sneezed—"Kertyshoo!" Mr. McGregor was after him in no time, and tried to put his foot upon Peter, who jumped out of a window, upsetting three plants. The window was too small for Mr. McGregor, and he was tired of running after Peter. He went back to his work.

Peter sat down to rest. He was out of breath and trembling with fright, and he had not the least idea which way to go. Also he was very damp with sitting in that can.

After a time he began to wander about, going lippity-lippity—not very fast, and looking all around.

He found a door in a wall, but it was locked, and there was no room for a fat little rabbit to squeeze underneath.

An old mouse was running in and out over the stone doorstep, carrying peas and beans to her family in the wood. Peter asked her the way to the gate, but she had such a large pea in her mouth that she could not answer. She only shook her head at him. Peter began to cry.

Then he tried to find his way straight across the garden, but he became more and more puzzled. Presently, he came to a pond where Mr. McGregor filled his water cans.

A white cat was staring at some goldfish. She sat very, very still, but now and then the tip of her tail twitched as if it were alive. Peter thought it best to go away without speaking to her. He had heard about cats from his cousin, little Benjamin Bunny.

He went back towards the tool shed, but suddenly quite close to him, he heard the noise of a hoe—*scr-r-ritch, scratch, scratch, scritch*. Peter scuttered underneath the bushes.

But presently, as nothing happened, he came out, and climbed upon a wheelbarrow, and peeped over. The first thing he saw was Mr. McGregor hoeing onions. His back was turned towards Peter, and beyond him was the gate!

Peter got down very quietly off the wheelbarrow, and started running as fast as he could go, along a straight walk behind some black currant bushes.

Mr. McGregor caught sight of him at the corner, but Peter did not care. He slipped underneath the gate and was safe at last in the wood outside the garden.

Mr. McGregor hung up the little jacket and the shoes for a scarecrow to frighten the blackbirds.

Peter never stopped running or looked behind him till he got home to the big fir tree.

He was so tired that he flopped down upon the nice soft sand on the floor of the rabbit-hold, and shut his eyes. His mother was busy cooking. She wondered what he had done with his clothes. It was the second little jacket and pair of shoes that Peter had lost in a fortnight!

I am sorry to say that Peter was not very well during the evening.

His mother put him to bed, and made some camomile tea. And she gave a dose of it to Peter!

"One tablespoonful to be taken at bedtime."

But Flopsy, Mopsy, and Cotton-tail had bread and milk and blackberries for supper.

Big Bird Brings Spring
to Sesame Street

By Lauren Collier Swindler
Illustrated by Marsha Winborn

Big Bird looked down Sesame Street. Everything was covered
with a thick layer of white snow. Big Bird sighed. It had been a
long winter. He was tired of looking at plain white snow.

Big Bird walked through the park and thought about all the
things he couldn't do because of the snow. He couldn't ride his
unicycle down Sesame Street. He couldn't play in the sandbox in
the playground. He couldn't roller-skate on the sidewalk.

"Besides, winter is so gloomy," thought Big Bird. "I wish
spring were here." Suddenly Big Bird had a wonderful idea. "I'll
buy some flowers to put in my nest. Then it will look like spring
is already here."

So Big Bird walked down to Mr. MacIntosh's store and bought six of his favorite flowers.

"I feel better already," thought Big Bird as he walked back toward Sesame Street with his bouquet of six beautiful flowers.

On the way to his nest, Big Bird stopped at the Count's castle.

"Ah, Big Bird, what beautiful flowers!" cried the Count. "Let me count them. One beautiful flower, two beautiful flowers, three, four, five, six beautiful flowers!

"Big Bird, I love counting your beautiful flowers."

"Gee, I didn't buy the flowers to count them," said Big Bird. "I bought them to remind me of spring. Would you like to keep this pretty pink daisy? You can count all of its petals."

"Wonderful!" cried the Count. "I also love counting flower petals. One pretty pink flower petal, two pretty pink flower petals, three . . ."

104

Big Bird walked down Sesame Street, carrying his five flowers. He stopped to watch Maria shovel snow from the sidewalk in front of the Fix-it Shop.

Oops! Maria slipped and fell in the snow.

"Oh, Maria, are you hurt?" asked Big Bird as he helped her stand up.

"No, Big Bird, I'm not hurt. But I am tired of winter and shoveling snow," she said.

"Here, Maria," said Big Bird. "You may have one of my flowers. It will help you feel happy again."

"Thank you, Big Bird," said Maria, taking the orange tiger lily.

Big Bird walked on down Sesame Street with the four flowers he had left. He found Grover sitting sadly on the steps.

"Oh, my goodness," said Grover unhappily. "Furry old Grover is very blue."

"Of course you are blue," said Big Bird. "You have blue fur."

"No, no, Big Bird. I mean that I am very sad," explained Grover. "I cannot ride my scooter in the snow."

"Maybe this blue pansy will make you feel better," said Big Bird, and he gave it to Grover.

Big Bird looked down at his three flowers, and he noticed that one of them was bent over. "Uh-oh," said Big Bird, holding up the purple iris. "This flower's stem is broken."

The lid of the trash can clanged open. "I love things that are broken!" said Oscar the Grouch, leaning out of his can.

"Well, gee, Oscar, I guess you may have my purple iris."

"Thanks, Bird," said Oscar. "Grouches like flowers that are bent and broken. Heh, heh, heh." He grabbed the purple iris and slammed down the lid of the trash can.

Big Bird clutched his last two flowers. Then he saw Ernie.

"Hi, Big Bird," said Ernie. "You look cold."

"I'm so cold, my tail feathers are frozen," answered Big Bird. "Where are you going?"

"I'm going to see Betty Lou. She's sick in bed with the flu. I wish I had something to take her to cheer her up. . . ."

"Oh," said Big Bird, looking down at his last two flowers. "Do you think she would like a yellow daffodil?"

"Oh, yes! Thank you, Big Bird." Ernie took the flower and went into 123 Sesame Street.

Big Bird went into Hooper's Store to get warm. Bert was sitting at the counter, sadly sipping his Figgy Fizz.

"What's wrong, Bert?" asked Big Bird. "You look kind of glum."

"I've lost my favorite paper clip," wailed Bert. "I dropped it in a snowdrift. Now I'll have to wait until the snow melts to find it. Oh, Big Bird, what if my paper clip gets all rusted by then?"

106

"Don't worry, Bert," said Big Bird. "Your paper clip will still be there in the spring."

"Ohhhhh, Big Bird!" said Bert with a sigh. Then he looked at the single rose Big Bird was holding. "Say, what are you going to do with that beautiful rose?" he asked.

"Uh, er . . . I'm going to give it to you, Bert." Big Bird gave Bert his last flower, and left Hooper's Store.

Empty-handed, Big Bird walked back up Sesame Street toward his nest. He had given away all six of his flowers. "Oh, well," he thought. "Soon it will be spring."

When he got to the lamppost, Big Bird turned around.

Sesame Street looked different! The plain white snow-covered street was splashed with bright colors. The flowers Big Bird had given to his friends were blooming up and down Sesame Street.

Big Bird had brought spring to Sesame Street.

The Cow Went Over the Mountain

By Jeanette Krinsley
Illustrated by Feodor Rojankovsky

One day Little Cow said to her mother, "I'm going over to the other mountain. The grass is munchier over there."

"Very well," said Mother Cow.

So away went Little Cow, and soon she met a little frog.

"Come along with me, Little Frog," she said. "I'm going over to the other mountain. The bugs are much crunchier there."

So Little Frog jumped up on Cow's back, and they walked along together. Soon they met a little white duck.

"Come with us," said Cow to Little White Duck. "We are going to the other mountain. The water is much sploshier there."

So Duck went, too.

Down the road they walked till they met a pig.

"Come along with us, Little Pig," said Cow. "We are going over to the other mountain. The mud is much sloshier there."

So Pig went, too, and they walked along together and sang a silly song.

"The grass is munchier.
The bugs are crunchier.
The water is sploshier.
The mud is sloshier."

Then they saw a bear, so they sang,

"The honey is gooier."

And Bear said, "I'll come, too."

And they walked and walked and walked.

When they got to the other mountain, they all sat down to rest. And they were so tired that they soon fell asleep.

In the morning they woke with the sun, very hungry and all ready to eat. BUT—

The grass was not munchier.

The bugs were not crunchier.

The water was not sploshier.

The mud was not sloshier.

The honey was not gooier.

It was just not true, all that Little Cow had said. And everyone felt sad and blue, till all at once Cow jumped up.

"Look," she said. "We are on the wrong mountain." And as she pointed they all agreed that the other mountain was greener.

So they started out again and walked and walked and walked.

Down, down, down they went till they came to the bottom of the mountain. Then—

Up, up, up they climbed. Then they stopped, and what do you think they found?

They were home, on their own green mountain. So they all
looked at Cow and sang—
   "The grass is munchier.
   The bugs are crunchier.
   The water is sploshier.
   The mud is sloshier.
   The honey is gooier,
   Right here at home."
And they laughed and laughed and laughed.

The Saggy Baggy Elephant

By Kathryn and Byron Jackson
Illustrated by Gustaf Tenggren

A happy little elephant was dancing through the jungle. He thought he was dancing beautifully, one-two-three-kick. But whenever he went one-two-three, his big feet pounded so that they shook the whole jungle. And whenever he went kick, he kicked over a tree or a bush.

The little elephant danced along, leaving wreckage behind him, until one day he met a parrot.

"Why are you shaking the jungle all to pieces?" cried the parrot, who had never before seen an elephant. "What kind of animal are you, anyway?"

The little elephant said, "I don't know what kind of animal I am. I live all alone in the jungle. I dance and I kick—I call myself Sooki. It's a good-sounding name, and it fits me, don't you think?"

"Maybe," answered the parrot, "but if it does, it's the only thing that *does* fit you. Your ears are too big for you, and your nose is way too big for you. And your skin is *much,* MUCH too big for you. It's baggy and saggy. You should call yourself Saggy–Baggy!"

Sooki sighed. His pants *did* look pretty wrinkled.

"I'd be glad to improve myself," he said, "but I don't know how to go about it. What shall I do?"

"I can't tell you. I never saw anything like you in all my life!" replied the parrot.

The little elephant tried to smooth out his skin. He rubbed it with his trunk. That did no good.

He pulled up his pants legs—
but they fell right back into
dozens of wrinkles.

It was very disappointing, and the parrot's saucy laugh didn't help a bit.

Just then a tiger came walking along. He was a beautiful, sleek tiger. His skin fit him like a glove.

Sooki rushed up to him and said:

"Tiger, please tell me why your skin fits so well! The parrot says mine is all baggy and saggy, and I do want to make it fit me like yours fits you!"

The tiger didn't care a fig about Sooki's troubles, but he did feel flattered and important, and he did feel just a little mite hungry.

"My skin always did fit," said the tiger. "Maybe it's because I take a lot of exercise. But . . ." added the tiger, ". . . if you don't care for exercise, I shall be delighted to nibble a few of those extra pounds of skin off for you!"

"Oh, no, thank you! No, thank you!" cried Sooki. "I love exercise! Just watch me!"

Sooki ran until he was well beyond reach.

Then he did somersaults and rolled on his back. He walked on his hind legs and he walked on his front legs.

115

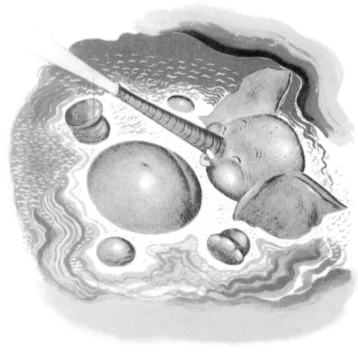

When Sooki wandered down to the river to get a big drink of water, he met the parrot. The parrot laughed harder than ever.

"I tried exercising," said the little elephant with a sigh. "Now I don't know what to do."

"Soak in the water the way the crocodile does," said the parrot, laughing. "Maybe your skin will shrink."

So Sooki tramped straight into the water.

But before he had soaked nearly long enough to shrink his skin, a great big crocodile came swimming up, snapping his fierce jaws and looking greedily at Sooki's tender ears.

The little elephant clambered up the bank and ran away, feeling very discouraged.

"I'd better hide in a dark place where my bags and sags and creases and wrinkles won't show," he said.

By and by he found a deep dark cave, and with a heavy sigh he tramped inside and sat down.

Suddenly he heard a fierce growling and grumbling and snarling. He peeped out of the cave and saw a lion padding down the path.

"I'm hungry!" roared the lion. "I haven't had a thing to eat today. Not a thing except a thin, bony antelope, and a puny monkey—and a buffalo, but such a tough one! And two turtles, but you can't count turtles. There's nothing much to eat between those saucers they wear for clothes! I'm *hungry*! I could eat an *elephant*!"

And he began to pad straight toward the dark cave where the little elephant was hidden.

"This is the end of me, sags, bags, wrinkles, and all," thought Sooki, and he let out one last trumpeting bellow!

Just as he did, the jungle was filled with a terrible crashing and an awful stomping. A whole herd of great gray wrinkled elephants came charging up, and the big hungry lion jumped up in the air, turned around, and ran away as fast as he could go.

Sooki peeped out of the cave and all the big elephants smiled at him. Sooki thought they were the most beautiful creatures he had ever seen.

"I wish I looked just like you," he said.

118

"You do," said the big elephants, grinning. "You're a perfectly dandy little elephant!"

And that made Sooki so happy that he began to dance one-two-three-kick through the jungle, with all those big, brave, friendly elephants behind him. The saucy parrot watched them dance. But this time he didn't laugh, not even to himself.

Hansel and Gretel

By The Brothers Grimm
Illustrated by Eloise Wilkin

On the edge of a small clearing, near a great forest, there lived a poor woodcutter and his wife and his two children, Hansel and Gretel. The wife was the children's stepmother, and she was very cruel to them.

They had always been very poor, but one time there was a great famine in the country, and the woodcutter could not earn even enough to buy any food for his family. The poor woodcutter worried day and night.

Finally he said to his wife, "What shall we do? We will surely starve. The food we have left is not enough for the children, let alone for us."

"I have a plan," the stepmother said.

120

"Early in the morning, we will take the children into the forest and leave them in the thickest part of it. They will never find their way home again, and we will be rid of them."

"I cannot do that!" cried the woodcutter.

But the cruel woman forced him to agree.

Now Hansel and Gretel heard them talking. And Hansel thought of a clever plan. Creeping outside, he filled his pockets with pebbles.

The next morning, before the sun was up, the stepmother shouted to the children, "Get up, you lazybones. We are going into the forest to cut wood. Here is a piece of bread. Don't eat it yet, because you won't get any more."

Then they set off for the forest, with Hansel and Gretel lagging in the rear. Gretel carried their bread, and Hansel stopped every few steps to drop a pebble on the ground.

Finally the father called back, "Hansel, hurry up! What's keeping you?"

"Oh, I'm just looking at my white kitten, who's sitting on the roof," said Hansel. "She's trying to say good-bye to me."

"You fool!" cried the stepmother. "That's the sunshine glinting on the roof."

When they reached the middle of the forest, the father built a good fire. Then the stepmother said, "Wait by the fire while we go to chop wood. We will come back to get you."

Hansel and Gretel fell asleep. When they woke up, it was night. Hansel comforted Gretel, who was frightened by the dark. Then, when the moon came up, they could see the pebbles that Hansel had dropped. And they followed them all the way home.

When they got home, the cruel stepmother planned again to get rid of them. And the next day they all went once more to the forest.

This time Hansel was not able to collect pebbles. He dropped bread crumbs instead.

But when evening came, they could not find the bread crumbs. The birds had eaten them. All night they walked, and all the next morning.

Suddenly they saw before them a little house, all made of gingerbread, with windows of spun sugar. They ran toward it eagerly.

Hansel ate a piece of the roof, and Gretel ate some of the window.

Then they heard a voice saying,

"Nibble, nibble, like a mouse,

Who is nibbling at my house?"

The children answered, "It's only the wind."

And they went on eating.

Then the door of the house opened, and an old woman came out, leaning on a crutch. The two children were very frightened, but the ugly old woman spoke very sweetly.

"Do come in," she said. "You must be very hungry and tired, for you look as if you've come a long way."

Then she led them into her house.

There she invited them to sit down to dinner. They were so hungry that they ate everything on the table.

When they had finished, the old woman put them to bed in great, comfortable beds.

Now, although the old woman seemed so kind, she was really a wicked witch who ate little children. So, while Hansel and Gretel were sleeping, she was thinking of the fine meal she would have.

The next morning she awakened Hansel and put him into a cage. No matter how he begged to get out, her heart did not soften. Then she woke up Gretel and put her to work.

"I'm going to eat you both," she said. "But first, you can do some of my work."

So poor Gretel had to carry water, chop kindling, scrub floors, and sweep the rooms.

Gretel did not get very much to eat, but the best kind of food was given to Hansel, for the witch thought he was too thin. Each morning she asked him to stretch out his finger, so she could feel how fat he was, for she could not see well. But Hansel stuck out an old bone, so she thought he was not growing any fatter.

At last the witch decided to eat him anyway.

Gretel had to build the fire and fill the kettle, and she cried as she worked.

Then the witch came to Gretel and said, "Crawl in the oven, Gretel, and see if it is hot enough."

But Gretel replied, "I don't know how to do it. How do I climb in the oven?"

"Stupid!" cried the witch. "The door is big enough. Why, I could get in myself!"

She bent down and put her head in the oven.

Quick as a flash, Gretel pushed her in and slammed the door! Then Gretel let Hansel out of his cage.

"Hansel, we're free!" she cried. "The old witch is dead!"

Filling their pockets with glittering jewels from the witch's hoard, they set off through the woods, determined to find their way home.

But though Hansel and Gretel walked and walked, they were still lost, and not a thing looked familiar.

Just when they had given up hope, they heard a happy cry. There was their father coming toward them.

"Hansel! Gretel!" cried the father, hurrying to them. "I have looked and looked for you."

He took them home, and Hansel and Gretel found that their cruel stepmother had gone away forever.

And with the jewels that they brought from the witch's house, they were able to live comfortably and happily ever after.

Walt Disney's
Donald Duck's Christmas Tree

It was the day before Christmas.

At Donald Duck's house, the cookies were all baked. The presents were all wrapped. It was time to get the Christmas tree.

Donald put on his coat and cap and mittens. He picked up his shiny ax.

"Come along, Pluto," he called. "We're going to the woods to find our Christmas tree." Pluto was visiting with Donald because Mickey was away for the holidays.

Pluto came on the run, and off they went into the snowy woods.

Now, deep in the woods in a sturdy fir tree lived two merry chipmunks, Chip 'n' Dale. They were getting ready for Christmas, too. They had found a tiny fir tree standing in the snow near their home. They were trimming it with berries and chains of dry grass when Donald and Pluto came along.

The chipmunks heard Donald whistling in the woods. Then they saw Pluto prancing at his side. They scampered home to safety. At least, they thought they were safe.

But Donald took one look at their sturdy tree and said, "This is just the tree for us!"

Chop, chop, chop went Donald's shiny ax. Poor Chip 'n' Dale were too frightened to think.

"Come on, Pluto," called Donald when the tree was down. "Let's take our tree home."

So through the woods went Donald Duck, whistling as he tramped along, dragging the fir tree home.

And among the branches sat Chip 'n' Dale, having a very nice ride.

Donald set up the tree in his living room as soon as he got home.

"There," he said when he was through. "It's time to trim the tree." Donald brought out boxes of ornaments.

From their hiding place up in the branches, Chip 'n' Dale looked on. They watched Donald loop long strings of colored lights over the branches of the tree.

They watched him hang bright-colored balls of gold and red and blue. Pluto helped where he could.

"There!" said Donald as he hung the last ball. "Doesn't that look fine?"

And indeed it was a beautiful Christmas tree.

"Now I'll pile everybody's presents under the tree," said
Donald. "Pluto, you stay here. I'll be right back."

"Bow-wow!" said Pluto as he sat down to admire the Christmas
tree.

As soon as Donald was out of sight, Chip 'n' Dale started to
have fun.

They danced on the branches until the needles quivered.

They made faces at themselves in the shiny colored balls and
laughed until their little sides shook.

"Grrr," growled Pluto disapprovingly.

But Chip 'n' Dale did not care. Chip just picked off two shiny balls and threw them at Pluto!

Pluto caught them in his paws.

"Grrr!" he growled crossly again.

Then Dale picked off another ball and threw it at Pluto, too!

Pluto jumped and barely caught it in his teeth. Just then, in walked Donald Duck.

"Pluto!" he cried. "Stop it!" He thought Pluto had been snatching balls from the tree.

Poor Pluto! There was not a sign of Chip 'n' Dale.

"Now, be good," said Donald, "while I bring in the rest of the presents."

No sooner had Donald gone than Chip 'n' Dale appeared once more. Plunk! Chip put a cracked plastic ball over his head. Dale laughed and laughed.

But Pluto did not think it was funny at all. They were spoiling Donald's tree!

"Grrr!" he growled, getting ready to jump.

"Pluto!" cried Donald Duck from the doorway. "What's the matter with you? Do you want to ruin the tree?"

Of course, Chip 'n' Dale were safely out of sight. Poor Pluto could not explain.

"Now you'll just have to go outside and stay in the yard for the rest of Christmas Eve," said Donald sternly.

But just then, up in the treetop, Chip grew tired of wearing his round golden mask. He pulled off the ball and let it drop.

Crash! It bounced off the floor.

"What was that?" cried Donald.

"Bow-wow!" said Pluto, pointing to the tree.

Dale began to play with the colored lights, twisting them so they turned on and off.

"What's this?" cried Donald Duck.

"Bow-wow! Bow-wow!" said Pluto, pointing again. Donald peered among the branches until he spied Chip 'n' Dale.

"Well, well," he said, chuckling as he lifted them down. "So you're the mischief-makers. And to think I blamed poor Pluto. I'm sorry, Pluto," said Donald.

Pluto marched over to the door and held it open. He thought
Chip 'n' Dale should go out in the snow.

"Oh, Pluto!" cried Donald. "It's Christmas Eve. We must be
kind to everyone, even pesky chipmunks. The spirit of Christmas is
love, you know."

So Pluto made friends with Chip 'n' Dale. They said they were
sorry, in chipmunk talk.

And when Donald's nephews, Huey, Dewey, and Louie, came
by to sing carols, eat cookies, and drink eggnog, they all agreed that
this was by far their happiest Christmas Eve ever.

We Like Kindergarten

By Clara Cassidy
Illustrated by Eloise Wilkin

My name is Carol.

I am going to kindergarten.

I go to kindergarten every day.

Laurie and Teddy Bear want to go to kindergarten, too.

So does Rusty.

So does Patches.

At kindergarten I hang up my spotted coat.

Stephen hangs up his brown coat.

All the boys and girls go into the kindergarten.

Miss Hall is our teacher.

She plays the piano.

We sing, "Good morning to you."

Michael feeds our fish.

Susan feeds our turtles.

We take turns.

Someday it will be my turn to feed them.

We do finger-painting.

I am painting with blue.

Karen is painting with red.

We make animals of clay.

I am making a dog.

Douglas is making an elephant.

We play games.

We play "Farmer in the Dell."
We play music.
Jack plays a drum.
Sally plays the bells.
We like to play music.
We listen while Miss Hall tells us stories.
We sit quietly.
We like to hear stories.
We show and tell about things that happen.
Mark told about his new baby sister.
Eric showed us his pet hamster.
We go outside to play.

I like to swing.

We all take turns.

We have milk to drink.

Jackie did not drink all of his milk.

We rest on our rugs.

My rug is blue.

Tim's rug is blue, too.

We dance.

Martha and Annette dance.

Paul and Jack dance.

We like to dance.

We draw pictures.

Miss Hall hangs our pictures on the wall.

I drew our house.

I drew a picture of Laurie by our house.

Now it's time to say good-bye.

"Good-bye, Miss Hall. See you tomorrow."

Laurie is waiting for me when I come home.

So is Rusty.

So is Patches.

And so is Teddy Bear.

Now I am the kindergarten teacher.

I am Miss Carol.

Laurie and Rusty and Patches are my boys and girls.

I play the piano.

The children sing, "Good morning to you."

Rusty and Patches and Teddy Bear sing softly.

Laurie sings loudly. She is glad to be in kindergarten.

The Sailor Dog

By Margaret Wise Brown
Illustrated by Garth Williams

Born at sea in the teeth of a gale, the sailor was a dog. Scuppers was his name.

After that he lived on a farm. But Scuppers, born at sea, was a sailor. And when he grew up, he wanted to go to sea.

So he went to look for something to go in.

He found a big airplane. "All aboard!" they called. It was going up in the sky. But Scuppers did not want to go up in the sky.

He found a little submarine. "All aboard!" they called. It was going down under the sea. But Scuppers did not want to go under the sea.

He found a little car.

"All aboard!" they called. It was going over the land. But Scuppers did not want to go over the land.

136

He found a subway train.

"All aboard!" they called. It was going under the earth. But Scuppers did not want to go under the earth.

Scuppers was a sailor. He wanted to go to sea.

So Scuppers went over the hills and far away until he came to the sea.

Over the hills and far away was the ocean. And on the ocean was a ship. The ship was about to go over the sea. It blew all its whistles.

"All aboard!" they called.

"All ashore that are going ashore!"

"All aboard!"

So Scuppers went to sea.

The ship began to move slowly along. The wind blew it.

In his ship Scuppers had a little room. In his room Scuppers had a hook for his hat and a hook for his rope and a hook for his handkerchief and a hook for his pants and a hook for his spyglass and a place for his shoes and a bunk for a bed to put himself in.

At night Scuppers threw the anchor into the sea and he went down to his little room.

He put his hat on the hook for his hat, and his rope on the hook for his rope, and his pants on the hook for his pants, and his spyglass on the hook for his spyglass, and he put his shoes under the bed, and got into his bed, which was a bunk, and went to sleep.

Next morning he was shipwrecked.

Too big a storm blew out of the sky. The anchor dragged and the ship crashed onto the rocks. There was a big hole in it.

Scuppers himself was washed overboard and hurled by huge waves onto the shore.

He washed up onto the beach. It was foggy and rainy. There were no houses and Scuppers needed a house.

But on the beach was lots and lots of driftwood, and he found an old rusty box stuck in the sand.

Maybe it was a treasure!

It was a treasure—to Scuppers.

It was an old-fashioned toolbox with hammers and nails and an ax and a saw. Everything he needed to build himself a house. So Scuppers started to build a house, all by himself, out of driftwood.

He built a door and
a window and a roof
and a porch and a floor,
all out of driftwood.

And he found some
red bricks and built a
big red chimney. And
then he lit a fire and the
smoke went up the
chimney.

After building his
house he was hungry. So
he went fishing.

He went fishing in a big river. The first fish he caught never
came up. The second fish he caught got away. The third fish he
caught was too little, but the next fish he caught was—just right.

Now he is cooking the fish he caught in the house he built, and
smoke is going up the chimney.

Then the stars came out and he was sleepy. So he built a bed of
pine branches.

And he jumped into his deep green bed and went to sleep. As
he slept he dreamed—

If he could build a house, he could mend the hole in the ship.

So the next day at low tide he took his toolbox and waded out
and hammered planks across the hole in his ship.

At last the ship was fixed.

So he sailed away.

Until he came to a seaport in a foreign land.

By now his clothes were all worn and ripped and torn and blown to pieces. His coat was torn, his hat was blown away, and his shoes were all worn out. And his handkerchief was ripped. Only his pants were still good.

So he went ashore to buy some clothes at the Army and Navy Store. And some fresh oranges. He bought a coat. He found a red one too small. He found a blue one just right. It had brass buttons on it.

Then he went to buy a hat. He found a purple one too silly. He found a white one just right.

He needed new shoes. He found some yellow ones too small. He found some red ones too fancy. Then he found some white ones just right.

Here he is with his new hat on, and with his new shoes on, and with his new coat on, with his shiny brass buttons. (He has a can of polish and a cloth to keep them shiny.)

And he has a new clean handkerchief, and a new rope, and a bushel of oranges.

And now Scuppers wants to go back to his ship. So he goes there.

And at night when the stars came out, he took one last look through his spyglass. And went down below to his little room, and he hung his new hat on the hook for the hat, and he hung his spyglass on the hook for his spyglass, and he hung his new coat on the hook for his coat, and his new handkerchief on the hook for his handkerchief, and his pants on the hook for his pants, and his new rope on the hook for his rope, and his new shoes he put under his bunk, and himself he put in his bunk.

And here he is where he wants to be—

A sailor sailing the deep green sea.

His Song

I am Scuppers the Sailor Dog—
I'm Scuppers the Sailor Dog—
I can sail in a gale
Right over a whale
Under full sail
In a fog.

I am Scuppers the Sailor Dog—
I'm Scuppers the Sailor Dog—
With a shake and a snort
I can sail into port
Under full sail
In a fog.

The Velveteen Rabbit

Adapted from the story by Margery Williams
Illustrated by Judith Sutton

There was once a velveteen rabbit, and in the beginning he was really splendid. He was fat and bunchy. His coat was brown and white, and his ears were lined with pink sateen. On Christmas morning he sat wedged in the top of the Boy's stocking, with a sprig of holly between his paws.

For at least two hours the Boy loved him, and then in the excitement of looking at all the new presents, the Velveteen Rabbit was forgotten.

For a long time the Velveteen Rabbit lived in the toy cupboard in the nursery. He was naturally shy, and some of the more expensive toys snubbed him.

The mechanical toys were very superior and pretended they were real. Even the jointed wooden lion put on airs.

Only the Skin Horse was kind to the Velveteen Rabbit. The Skin Horse was very wise and had lived longer in the nursery than any of

144

the other toys. He knew that nursery magic is very strange and wonderful, and only those playthings that are very old and experienced can understand it.

"What is REAL?" the Rabbit asked the Skin Horse one day. "Does it mean having things that buzz inside you and a stick-out handle?"

"Real isn't how you are made," said the Skin Horse. "It's a thing that happens to you. It takes a long, long time. That's why it doesn't often happen to toys that break easily, or who have sharp edges, or have to be carefully kept. When a child REALLY loves you, then you become Real."

"I suppose you are REAL?" asked the Rabbit.

The Skin Horse smiled. "The Boy's uncle made me Real many years ago," he said. "And once you are Real, you can't become unreal again. It lasts for always."

The Rabbit sighed. He thought it would be a long time before this magic thing called Real happened to him.

One evening, when the Boy was going to bed, he couldn't find the toy dog that always slept with him. So Nana gave him the Velveteen Rabbit instead.

That night, and for many nights after, the Velveteen Rabbit slept in the Boy's bed.

At first the Rabbit found it rather uncomfortable. Then he grew to like it, for the Boy made nice tunnels for him under the bedclothes. The Boy said they were like the burrows the real rabbits lived in. And when the Boy dropped off to sleep, the Rabbit would snuggle down under the Boy's warm little chin and dream.

And so time went on. The little Rabbit was so happy that he never noticed how his beautiful velveteen fur was getting shabbier, and his tail was coming unsewn, and all the pink was rubbing off his nose where the Boy kissed him.

When Spring came, the Rabbit had rides in the wheelbarrow, picnics on the grass, and fairy huts built just for him under the raspberry bush.

And once when the Boy was called away suddenly, and the Rabbit was left out on the lawn until long after dusk, Nana had to go and look for him because the Boy couldn't sleep unless he was there.

"Fancy all that fuss for a toy!" said Nana.

The Boy sat up in bed. "He isn't a toy," he said. "He's REAL!"

When the little Rabbit heard that, he was happy, for he knew that what the Skin Horse had said was true at last. He was a toy no longer. He was Real! The Boy himself had said so.

One summer evening the Rabbit saw two strange beings creep out of the woods. They were rabbits like himself, but quite furry and brand-new. They must have been very well made, for their seams didn't show, and they changed shape when they moved.

They stared at him, and the little Rabbit stared back. And all the time their noses twitched.

"Why don't you get up and play with us?" one of them asked.

"I don't feel like it," said the Velveteen Rabbit.

"Can you hop on your hind legs?" asked the other furry rabbit.

"I don't want to," answered the Velveteen Rabbit.

One of the rabbits came up very close and sniffed.

"He hasn't got any hind legs!" the furry rabbit called out. "And he doesn't smell right! He isn't a rabbit at all! He isn't real!"

"I *am* Real!" said the little Rabbit. "The Boy said so!"

But just then there was a sound of footsteps, and the Boy ran

past the furry rabbits. With a stamp of feet and a flash of white, the
two strange rabbits disappeared.

For a long time the little Rabbit sat very still, hoping the two
rabbits would come back to play with him. But they never returned.
The sun sank lower, and the Boy came to carry him home.

Then one day the Boy grew ill. His face grew flushed, he talked
in his sleep, and his little body was so hot that it burned the Rabbit
when he held him close.

It was a long, weary time, for the Boy was too ill to play. But the
little Rabbit snuggled down patiently and looked forward to the time
when they would play in the garden and the woods like they used to.

At last the fever turned, and the Boy got better. The doctor
ordered that all the books and toys that the Boy had played with be
burned. So the little Rabbit was put into a sack and carried out to the
garden.

Nearby he could see the raspberry bush that he had played in
with the Boy. He thought of the Skin Horse and all that he had been
told by him. Of what use was it to be loved and become Real if it all
ended like this? And a tear, a real tear, trickled down his shabby
velvet nose and fell to the ground.

147

And then a strange thing happened. For where the tear had fallen, a flower grew out of the ground. And out of that flower stepped a fairy. She came close to the little Rabbit and kissed him on his velveteen nose.

"Little Rabbit, don't you know who I am?" she asked. The Rabbit looked up at her, and it seemed to him that he had seen her face before, but he couldn't think of where.

"I am the nursery magic Fairy," she said. "I take care of all the playthings that children have loved. When the children don't need them anymore, I turn them into Real."

"Wasn't I Real before?" asked the little Rabbit.

"You were Real to the Boy," the Fairy said, "because he loved you. Now you shall be Real to everyone."

Then the Fairy took the Rabbit up in her arms and flew away with him into the woods.

The woods were beautiful, and the ferns shone like frosted silver. In the clearing the wild rabbits danced, but when they saw the Fairy, they all stopped dancing and stood around in a ring to stare at her.

"I've brought you a new playmate," the Fairy told them. "You must be very kind to him, for he is going to live with you forever and ever!" Then she kissed the little Rabbit again and said, "Run and play, little Rabbit!"

The little Rabbit sat quite still for a moment. He did not know that when the Fairy had kissed him, she had changed him altogether. He might have sat there for a long time, if just then something hadn't tickled his nose, and he lifted his leg to scratch it.

And he found that he actually had hind legs! Instead of velveteen, he had brown fur, soft and shiny, and his ears twitched by themselves.

He gave one leap, and the joy of using those hind legs was so great, he went springing about—jumping sideways and whirling around as the others did. He grew so excited that when he did stop to look for the Fairy, she had gone.

He was a Real Rabbit at last!

Autumn passed, and Winter, and in the Spring, the Boy went out to play in the woods. While he was playing, two rabbits crept out and peeped at him. One of them had strange markings under his fur, as though long ago he had been stuffed.

The Boy thought to himself, "Why, he looks just like my old Bunny that was lost!"

But he never knew that it really was his own Bunny, who had come back to look at the child who had first helped him to be Real.

Walt Disney's

101 Dalmatians

Adapted by Justine Korman
Illustrated by Bill Langley and Ron Dias

Pongo, Perdita, and their fifteen puppies lived in a cozy little house in London. Their humans lived there, too: Roger, who was tall and thin and played the piano, and Anita, who laughed a lot. They all got along splendidly and were very happy.

Then one day the doorbell rang, and in came Cruella De Vil, Anita's old friend from school.

"I'm so glad the puppies have finally gotten their spots!" Cruella said, stroking their soft fur. "I'll pay for them now."

"Pay for the puppies?" gasped Anita. "Oh, Cruella, we couldn't part with them."

"Don't be silly, Anita," said Cruella. "You can't possibly keep fifteen puppies."

"We are not selling them," said Roger, "and that's final!"

Furious, Cruella stamped out of the house.

One frosty night a few weeks later, Pongo and Perdita went out for a walk with Roger and Anita. The puppies were at home, asleep in their basket.

Suddenly two men burst into the house. They put all the puppies into a big bag. Then they carried the bag out to their truck and sped away.

After being in the truck for what seemed like hours, the fifteen puppies found themselves in a room filled with many other

Dalmatian puppies. On a couch in front of a television set were the two nasty men who had kidnapped them.

The other Dalmatians told them that the men worked for Cruella De Vil, who had bought the puppies from pet stores.

Back at home, Pongo and Perdita were horrified to find their puppies missing.

"It's that evil Cruella De Vil," Perdita said, sobbing. "She has stolen our puppies! Oh, Pongo, do you think we'll ever find them?"

"I have a plan," said Pongo. "Let's try the Twilight Bark." The Twilight Bark was a system of long and short barks used by dogs to pass along news.

The next evening Pongo and Perdita went on another walk with Roger and Anita. While the Dalmatians were out, they barked long and loud. They wanted all the dogs in London to be on the lookout for their puppies.

Pongo waited for someone to answer his barks. It was a very cold night, and most dogs were inside. Then Perdita added her bark to Pongo's, and at last they heard a reply.

"Message received. Most sorry about your puppies. Will do all I can to help spread the word," howled a Great Dane.

That night the Twilight Bark even reached a quiet farm where an old sheepdog known as the Colonel lay sleeping.

"Alert, alert!" shouted Sergeant Tibs, a cat who lived on the farm. "Vital message coming in from London."

The Colonel lifted one shaggy ear to listen to the faint message. "Fifteen puppies have been stolen!" he cried.

"I heard puppies barking at the old De Vil mansion," said Tibs. "You don't suppose . . ."

The Colonel barked a message back to London. Then he told Tibs, "We should investigate right away!"

They headed straight for the
gloomy De Vil mansion. Tibs held
on tight to the Colonel's back as he
rushed through the snow.

Once they arrived, Tibs climbed
up onto the Colonel's shoulders. He
peeked through an open window.

"Good night!" said the cat when he saw all the puppies. "There
are a whole lot of you. I'm looking for fifteen puppies who were
stolen from London."

"I was stolen!" cried Lucky, one of the puppies. "And so were
my brothers and sisters."

The men heard the noise and went to investigate. Tibs and the
Colonel ran away, but not before promising to get help.

The next morning Cruella De Vil arrived in her car.

"It's got to be done today!" she cried.

"But you couldn't get a dozen coats out of the
whole caboodle," protested one of her men,
pointing to the puppies.

"Then I'll have to settle for
half a dozen," said Cruella.
"Just do it!"

She dashed out, then roared off in her car.

Sergeant Tibs and the Colonel had returned just in time to hear Cruella give the order. "You kids had better get out of here before they make coats out of you," Tibs whispered. Then he shoved one of the puppies toward a hole in the wall.

"It's too small," protested the pup.

"Squeeze!" ordered Tibs, and the puppy got through.

One by one the other puppies followed.

Suddenly the two thugs realized that the puppies were escaping. The chase was on! Tibs and the puppies scooted through the dark halls of the mansion. Soon they found themselves trapped at a dead end. The thugs raised their clubs to strike.

At that moment Pongo and Perdita crashed through the window with a blast of glass and freezing air. The angry Dalmatian parents fought off the astonished men as all the puppies scampered to safety.

Once the dogs were safely outside, they thanked the Colonel and Tibs and said good-bye. Then they hurried toward London.

Pongo and Perdita led the way, their fifteen puppies and all the other Dalmatian pups right behind them.

When they reached a frozen stream, they carefully crossed the slippery surface so they wouldn't leave paw prints. Then they resumed the race home.

All along the route the Dalmatians were helped by other dogs. A black Labrador retriever arranged for them to ride to London in a moving van. The Dalmatians waited in a shed while the van was being fixed.

Suddenly Cruella's big car pulled up outside. Somehow she had followed their tracks.

"Oh, Pongo," said Perdita. "How will we get to the van?"

Pongo noticed lots of ashes in the fireplace. If they all rolled in the soot, they would look just like black Labradors.

When the van was ready, the dogs marched outside. One after another, the soot-covered puppies were lifted into the van. Before Pongo had a chance to pick up the last one, a clump of snow fell from the shed onto the puppy.

Pongo snatched up the pup, but the snow had washed away the soot. From her car, Cruella could see the white fur and black spots.

"They're escaping!" she shouted as the van moved away.

Faster and faster went the van, but Cruella's car drew closer and closer. She was screaming in anger. Then she began to yell in fear.

Her car skidded on the icy road. Cruella tried to stop it, but her car spun around and slid into a ditch.

The last the Dalmatians saw of Cruella, she was standing beside her wrecked car, having a nasty temper tantrum.

When the van reached the cozy little house in London, Roger and Anita were overjoyed. And when they counted the dogs, they discovered that they now had 101 Dalmatians!

"We'll have to buy a big house in the country," said Roger. "We'll have a Dalmatian plantation!"

And they did exactly that. Pongo, Perdita, and all the spotted puppies lived there happily ever after.

Seven Little Postmen

By Margaret Wise Brown and Edith Thacher Hurd
Illustrated by Tibor Gergely

A boy had a secret. It was a surprise.
He wanted to tell his grandmother.
So he sent his secret through the mail.
The story of that letter
Is the reason for this tale
Of the seven little postmen who carried the mail.

Because there was a secret in the letter
The boy sealed it with red sealing wax.
If anyone broke the seal,
The secret would be out.
He slipped the letter into the mailbox.

The first little postman
Took it from the box,
Put it in his bag,
And walked seventeen blocks
To a big Post Office
All built of rocks.

The letter with the secret
Was dumped on a table
With big and small letters
That all needed the label
Of the big Post Office.

Stamp stamp, clickety-click,
The machinery ran with a quick sharp tick.
The letter with the secret is stamped at last
And the round black circle tells that it passed
Through the canceling machine
Whizz whizz fast!

Big letters
Small letters
Thin and tall—
The second little postman
Sorts them all.
The letters are sorted
From East to West
From North to South.

"And this letter
Had best go West,"
Said the second
Little postman,
Scratching his chest.
Into the pouch
Lock it tight
The secret letter
Must travel all night.

The third little postman in the big mail car
Comes to a crossroad where waiting are
A green, a yellow, and a purple car.
They all stop there. There is nothing to say.
The mail truck has the right of way!
"The mail must go through!"

Up and away through sleet and hail
This airplane carries the fastest mail.
The pilot flies through whirling snow
As far and as fast as the plane can go.

And he drops the mail for the evening train.
Now hang the pouch on the big hook crane!

The engine speeds up the shining rails
And the fourth little postman
Grabs the mail with a giant hook.
The train roars on
With a puff and a snort
And the fourth little postman
Begins to sort.

The train carries the letter
Through gloom of night
In a mail car filled with
      electric light
To a country postman
By a country road
Where the fifth little postman
Is waiting for his load.

The mail clerk
Heaves the mail pouch
With all his might
To the fifth little postman
Who grabs it tight.

Then off he goes
Along the lane
And over the hill
Until
He comes to a little town
That is very small—
So very small
The Post Office there
Is hardly one at all.

160

The sixth little postman
In great big boots
Sorts the letters
For their various routes—
Some down the river,
Some over the hill.
But the secret letter
Goes farther still.

The seventh little postman on R.F.D.
Carries letters and papers,
    chickens and fruit
To the people who live
    along his route.

He stops to deliver some sugar
To Mr. Jones, who keeps a store
And always seems to need
    something more.
For Mrs. O'Finnigan with all her ills
He brings a bottle of bright pink pills.
And an airmail letter that cost six cents
He hands to a farmer over the fence.

There was a special
Delivery—crisp orange
And blue. What was the
Hurry, nobody knew.

There were parts
For a tractor
And a wig for an actor,

And a funny postcard
For a little boy
Playing in his own backyard.

There was something for Sally
And something for Sam
And something for Mrs. Potter
Who was busy making jam.

There were dozens of chickens
For Mrs. Pickens
And a dress for a party
For Mrs. McCarty.

At the last house along the way sat the grandmother of the boy who had sent the letter with the secret in it. She had been wishing all day he would come to visit. For she lived all alone in a tiny house and sometimes felt quite lonely.

The postman blew his whistle and gave her the letter with the red sealing wax on it—the secret letter!

"Sakes alive! What is it about?" Sakes alive! The secret is out! What does it say?

DEAREST GRANNY:
I AM WRITING TO SAY
THAT I'M COMING TO VISIT ON SATURDAY.
MY CAT HAS SEVEN KITTENS AND I AM BRINGING
ONE TO YOU FOR YOUR VERY OWN KITTEN.
THE POSTMAN IS #5 MY FRIEND.
                    YOUR GRANDSON
                         THOMAS

Seven Little Postmen

Seven Little Postmen carried the mail
Through Rain and Snow and Wind and Hail
Through Snow and Rain and Gloom of Night

    Seven Little Postmen
    Out of sight.
    Over Land and Sea
    Through Air and Light
    Through Snow and Rain
    And Gloom of Night—
    Put a stamp on your letter
    And seal it tight.

Tommy Visits the Doctor

By Jean H. Seligmann and Milton I. Levine, M.D.
Illustrated by Richard Scarry

Today Tommy is going to visit Doctor Brown.
   Doctor Brown is not a doctor for mommies.
   He is not a doctor for daddies.
   Doctor Brown is a doctor for children.
   Doctor Brown is Tommy's doctor.
   *And Bobby Bunny is
going to visit Doctor Smiles.*
   *Doctor Smiles is a
doctor for bunnies.*

   Tommy is not sick.
   Tommy wants to show Doctor Brown how big he is growing. He wants Doctor Brown to see how strong he is.
   And Bobby wants Doctor Smiles to see how well he is.

   Tommy rings the doorbell at the doctor's office. Doctor Brown's nurse opens the door and smiles at Tommy.
   "Come in, Tommy," she says. "Doctor Brown will be ready to see you in a few minutes."
   Bobby's doctor has a nice nurse, too.

   Tommy sees his friend Sally in the waiting room.
   She has just been to see the doctor.
   "Hi, Tommy," says Sally. "I have grown two inches since last time."

"That's great!" says Tommy.
Bobby's friend Fluffy says, "I'm one whole pound heavier!"

Tommy rides on the rocking horse.
And Bobby plays with a red truck.

Soon Doctor Brown comes out and says, "Hello, Tommy, come in. It's your turn now."
They go into Doctor Brown's office.
"Now, Tommy," says Doctor Brown, "the first thing you do is take off your shoes and socks and shirt and slacks."
Bobby takes off his clothes, too.

"Now let's get up on the scale and see how heavy you are."
Doctor Brown looks at the scale and says, "You weigh forty pounds. That's five pounds more than the last time you were here! Your mommy must be feeding you well."
"My," says Doctor Smiles, "what a fine big rabbit you are!"
"I eat all my carrots," says Bobby proudly.

"Did you grow taller, too?" asks Doctor Brown.
"Yes," says Tommy. "Last year's coat is too short."
"Let's see how much you grew," says Doctor Brown. "Stand as tall as you can."
Doctor Brown measures Tommy.
"Indeed you did grow!" says Doctor Brown. "You grew this much."

Bobby Bunny has grown, too.
"Especially your ears," says Doctor Smiles.

"Now hop on this table," says Doctor Brown. "I'm going to look into your ears." He takes out something that looks like a flashlight with a tiny light at the end of it.

"First let's look in this ear. Now the other.

"Good," says Doctor Brown. "You've got two fine ears."

Bobby's ears are much bigger than Tommy's.

That's because Bobby has rabbit ears.

"And now," says Doctor Brown, "I'm going to look into your mouth and count your teeth. 1, 2, 3, 4, 5, 6, 7, 8, 9, 10 on the top, and 1, 2, 3, 4, 5, 6, 7, 8, 9, 10 on the bottom. That's twenty teeth, and just right for your age. Be sure you take good care of them."

Bobby has just enough teeth for a healthy little rabbit.

"Next," says Doctor Brown, "I want to look way down your throat. Can you open your mouth very, very wide? That's fine. And now, while your mouth is open, stick out your tongue and say 'A–a–a–ah.' That's very good. Your throat looks fine."

Doctor Smiles looks down Bobby's throat, too.

Tommy lies down on the table, and Doctor Brown goes thump-thump-thump all over Tommy's chest.

He does the same thing on Tommy's back. It sounds like a little drum.

Bobby laughs when Doctor Smiles goes thump-thump. He is a tickly rabbit.

"Now I will use my stethoscope," says Doctor Brown.

"What is it for?" asks Tommy.

"It makes things sound louder," says Doctor Brown. "Here—you can listen to my heart with it."

Tommy hears Doctor Brown's heart going boom-boom-boom-boom.

And Bobby hears Doctor Smiles's heart go bumpity-bumpity-bump!

Then Doctor Brown puts the stethoscope in his ears and listens to Tommy's heart.

"You sound just fine, young man," he tells Tommy.

"You sound just fine, young rabbit," says Doctor Smiles.

Tommy lies down again, and Doctor Brown feels his stomach.

Tommy is very ticklish. He can't help giggling.

Bobby giggles, too, and wiggles his ears.

"Now sit up, Tommy, and dangle your legs over the table," says Doctor Brown. "If I hit the right spot on the knee, your foot jumps up all by itself. Watch."

He taps Tommy's knee very lightly with a little rubber hammer, and Tommy's foot jumps up.

"Look, my foot jumps up by itself," says Bobby. "Do it again!"

"Now," says Doctor Brown, "how well can you see? I'll show you some pictures."

"That's a star!" says Tommy.

He looks at more pictures, and he knows what every one of them is.

"Good!" says Doctor Brown. "You see very well."

Doctor Smiles shows Bobby pictures, too.

Doctor Brown looks at a card that has Tommy's name at the top.

"I see you need a shot this time, Tommy."

"What is a shot like?" asks Tommy.

"It feels like a quick pinprick, and it's over in a second," says Doctor Brown. "This shot will keep you well and strong."

Bobby needs a shot, too.

Tommy holds out his arm. The doctor rubs Tommy's skin with a piece of cotton wet with alcohol.

"That's to make sure your skin is clean," says the doctor. "By the time you take a deep breath, the shot will be over." And it is!

"That wasn't so bad," says Bobby.

Just then the nurse comes in with some lollipops. "Choose one!" she tells Tommy.

"Thank you," says Tommy. "I'll take a red one!"

Bobby's nurse gives him a yellow balloon.

"All right, Tommy, you can get dressed now," says Doctor Brown. "You are a very healthy boy. When you come again, we'll see how much more you have grown."

Tommy and his mother say good-bye to the doctor.

Bobby gets dressed.

"Good-bye, Doctor Smiles," says Bobby.

Tommy can hardly wait to get home.

He wants to tell his daddy how much he has grown.

"How pleased Daddy will be!" says Mommy.

"What a fine healthy bunny I have," says Mr. Rabbit.

168

The Pied Piper

Retold by Alan Benjamin
Illustrated by Richard Walz

Based on a poem by Robert Browning

The town of Hamelin lay along the bank of a wide river. Its twisting streets were lined with the comfortable houses of the happy people who lived there. Life had gone on peacefully and pleasantly in Hamelin for as long as anyone could remember.

And then one day *rats* began to appear. At first there were only a few, and no one minded very much. In fact, the town's cats couldn't have been happier. But the rats multiplied, and soon there were more rats than townsfolk.

The rats were everywhere. After a while, folks didn't even feel safe in their own homes. The rats ate everything they could find.

Sometimes people were awakened in the middle of the night by rats about to nibble on their toes!

Finally the people of Hamelin were at their wits' end. Off they marched to the town hall to see the mayor. The mayor was a greedy man. He cared a great deal about money but very little about Hamelin's citizens.

"The rats are eating us out of house and home!" cried an angry woman in the crowd.

The mayor told the townspeople to be patient, that he was doing all he could to help.

"Get rid of the rats—and soon—or we'll get rid of you!" shouted the town's banker.

The mayor was upset. Later, when he met with his council members, one of them said, "We've tried poison and traps, but we haven't caught any rats."

"Well, think of something that *will* work," the mayor thundered, "or we'll all be out of our jobs!"

Suddenly there was a tapping at the door. In stepped the oddest-looking fellow any of the council members had ever seen. He was as tall and as lean as a birch tree, with long sharp features and bright eyes as blue as sapphires. His clothes were a marvelous patchwork of color, and in his hand he carried a musical pipe.

"Who are you?" barked the mayor.

"I'm only a poor piper," answered the stranger, "but I can pipe music that will charm any living creature. If you will pay me a thousand guilders, I will get rid of the rats."

170

"If you can really do as you say, I'll give you fifty thousand guilders!" cried the mayor.

"Then play I shall," said the piper as he stepped outside. He raised his pipe to his lips, and out came a melody both strange and beautiful. No one had ever heard music quite like it.

As the piper piped, out came the rats—big ones and small ones, fat ones and thin ones—till Hamelin's streets were filled with them. The rats followed the piper as he made his way through town, while the people watched in wonder.

When the piper came to the bank of the river, he stopped, but he continued to play his pipe. The rats, however, did not stop. Into the river they plunged—never to return to the town.

Hamelin was free of vermin at last. The people cheered as the piper made his way back to the town hall.

"I've come to collect my thousand guilders," he told the mayor.

"But I was only joking," said the mayor, chuckling. Now that the rats were gone, he had no further need for the piper. "I'll give you these fifty guilders and nothing more. Now take them and leave."

"Then leave I shall," said the piper, "but not before I've played a different tune." And he stepped outside and lifted his pipe once more.

As the music began, the pattering of feet could be heard. But this time it was not the rats. From every corner of Hamelin came the children of the town. Hand in hand, dancing and prancing, the children followed the piper as he led them through the town.

When parents recognized their children in the procession, they tried to stop them but could not. The music had frozen the parents in place like statues.

On went the piper and his army of children, through the streets and over the bridge that led out of town. The last in line was a little lame boy. The tapping of his cane as he hurried to keep up with the others was the last sound the stricken townsfolk heard as their children disappeared from view.

When they could move again, the townsfolk rushed across the bridge to find the children. Following the road that led from Hamelin, they soon came to a mountain that the children had climbed.

There they found the little lame boy in tears. He told them that when the piper and the children had reached this place, a door in the mountain had opened up, and everyone had entered. Everyone, that is, except the boy himself. "I could not keep up with the others," he told the grown-ups sadly. "The door closed before I could reach it."

"Did the piper say where he was taking our children?" someone asked.

"Yes," the boy replied. "To a happy land where it is always spring. To a land of flowers and fountains, peacocks and winged horses."

The people stood and wept. Some pleaded with the mountain to open. Others shouted for the piper to return, promising that the mayor would pay what was owed him—and more.

But the mountain did not open, and the piper did not answer.

Let us all, dear reader, think well before we make promises we do not plan to keep. If, in our greed, we give less than we promised, we may get more than we bargained for.

173

Walt Disney's
Mickey and the Beanstalk

Adapted by Dina Anastasio
Illustrated by Sharon Ross

Far, far away, where the trees were greener than the prettiest green and the sky was bluer than the brightest blue, there was a place called Happy Valley. In Happy Valley the brooks babbled, the birds sang, and everyone smiled all day long.

The farmers whistled and hummed as they did their chores. Children sang as they skipped to school. In Happy Valley every day was a happy day.

High on a hill, overlooking Happy Valley, stood a magnificent castle. In the castle was the Golden Harp, who sang all day and cast a magic spell of happiness over the land.

But one day a terrible thing happened in Happy Valley. Someone stole the Golden Harp from the castle, and the magic spell of happiness was gone.

The birds stopped singing. The brooks stopped babbling. The crops stopped growing. The cows stopped giving milk. And all the people of Happy Valley grew sad and hungry.

"We must do something," said Farmer Donald.

"We'll starve if we don't," added Farmer Goofy.

"I know!" said Farmer Mickey. "I'll sell Bossy the cow and buy some food."

Mickey took the cow into town and sold her. When he returned, he said, "I have sold Bossy for three wonderful beans."

"Three beans!" cried Donald and Goofy. "We can't live on three beans!" Donald threw the beans on the floor in disgust.

"But . . . but . . . they are magic beans," said Mickey as he sadly watched the beans roll through a crack in the floor.

But Goofy and Donald didn't pay any attention to what Mickey was saying. They were too tired and hungry to listen.

During the night a moonbeam shone through the window and through the crack in the floor onto the beans.

The beans sprouted and began to grow. They grew into a stalk that lifted the house. The beanstalk climbed all the way up to the sky.

In the morning the hungry farmers woke up and looked out the window.

To their surprise Happy Valley was gone! All they could see from their window was a tremendous castle.

"Let's go!" said Mickey. "Whoever lives in that big castle must have plenty of food to share!"

Mickey, Donald, and Goofy climbed up to the top of the castle stairs and crawled under the front door. On an enormous table they saw huge platters of food. Mammoth pitchers of fresh cold milk waited for them. The farmers quickly climbed up a table leg and ate, drank, and laughed merrily.

As they were finishing their meal, a tiny voice called out to them.

"Who's that?" asked Mickey.

"It came from in there," said Donald, pointing to a box that was on the table.

Mickey, Donald, and Goofy moved closer to the box. "Who are you?" they asked.

"It is I, the Golden Harp," said a soft voice. "A giant kidnapped me and brought me here to his castle to sing for him."

The farmers were very frightened to hear that the castle belonged to a giant. They were so frightened that they almost ran away.

"Wait!" cried Mickey suddenly. "We can't leave without the Golden Harp."

"You're right," said Goofy bravely. "We have to rescue her and save Happy Valley!"

Just then they heard loud footsteps. Everything in the room was shaking as the footsteps came closer and closer.

"You must hide!" cried the Golden Harp.

Mickey, Donald, and Goofy ran as quickly as they could to hide from the evil giant.

The giant stomped over to the table and picked up a giant sandwich in his giant hand. He was just about to take a bite when he noticed that the sandwich was moving.

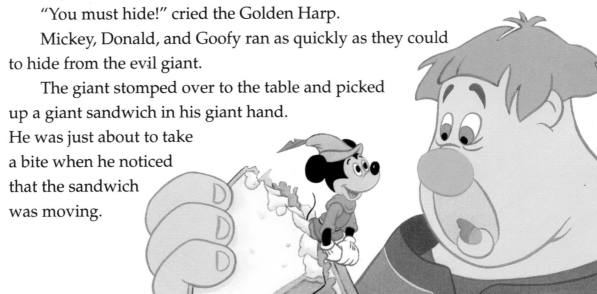

"There's a mouse in my sandwich!" roared the giant.

"Oh, I'm sorry," said Mickey. "I had no idea this was your sandwich." He jumped from the sandwich to the giant's shirt and then slid down the giant's leg.

"Run!" shouted Mickey to Donald and Goofy.

The giant was furious. He chased the three farmers around the room until they were cornered. The giant reached down to scoop them up in his hand—but he missed Mickey!

The great big giant put the tiny little farmers into the box with the Golden Harp. He locked the box and slipped the key into his great big pocket. Then he sat down in a chair to take a nap.

Mickey waited in his hiding place behind the pitcher. When the giant finally fell asleep, Mickey tiptoed over to the box and knocked.

"The key," whispered the Golden Harp. "Get the key out of his pocket."

Mickey hurried over to the sleeping giant. Very slowly and carefully he pulled the key out of the giant's pocket.

The giant mumbled something and stirred, but he did not wake up.

Mickey tiptoed back to the box and unlocked it. Goofy and Donald climbed out and then quickly lifted out the Golden Harp. The four were very quiet as they made their way to the front door.

Just as they were sneaking past the giant, he opened one eye and let out a giant roar.

Goofy and Donald ran with the Golden Harp in their arms. Mickey realized the giant would catch them unless he could do something to distract him.

"You can't catch me!" Mickey taunted. The angry giant ran toward Mickey, who dived under a rug. "Over here!" Mickey said, but the giant was not fast enough to catch Mickey.

Mickey ran toward an open window. "So long!" he shouted as he jumped outside.

Mickey ran to the beanstalk, with the giant following close behind. He jumped on the beanstalk and slid down in a flash.

Donald and Goofy grabbed a saw and cut down the beanstalk in the nick of time. The giant fell and crashed through the ground, all the way to the center of the earth.

The farmers took the Golden Harp back to her castle to sing, and from that time on, Happy Valley was happy once again. And happiest of all were the three brave farmers—Mickey, Donald, and Goofy!

What's Next, Elephant?

By Kathryn and Byron Jackson

Illustrated by Feodor Rojankovsky

Formerly titled *The Big Elephant*

Once upon a time there was a great, enormous, huge, and very big elephant who traveled with the circus.

He just loved to dress up in all his splendid circus clothes.

And he loved to march into the big tent and do all his fine big tricks. Then the circus band played its wonderful music, the lights shone and sparkled, and the crowd clapped and cheered.

The big elephant felt so happy that he chose a partner and waltzed round and round the center ring.

"What a fine life it is!" he cried.

But at night the circus moved from one town to another. The train whistled and tooted and rocked and swayed all night long.

Whenever the great, enormous, huge, and very big elephant turned over in his sleep, out he fell, into the aisle.

He never did get enough sleep.

And one night he fell out three times!

The very next morning he said good-bye to all his circus friends.

"I'm going to live in a house with a great, enormous, huge, and very low bed," he said.

He hopped off the train the minute it slowed down and hailed the first bus that came along.

Soon the big elephant found himself in the middle of a busy town. There was a bakery on one corner, a ten-cent store across the street, and a roller-skating rink on another corner.

It was hard to decide what to do first!

But at last the big elephant made up his mind.

"First," he said, "I will build my house."

It was great fun sawing and hammering, and talking to the children who had come to watch.

Their parents came, too.

"We'll give you a hand," they said.

With all that help, it took no time to finish the house—great, enormous, huge, and very low bed and all.

"It's cozy and fine and exactly right!" cried the big elephant.

He thanked all his new friends over and over again.

Then he rolled into his bed, which suited him perfectly, and slept right around the clock.

In the morning his new house pleased him more than ever. The big elephant thought he had not thanked his new friends nearly enough. So he dressed in his best and hurried into town.

"Good morning," he said to everyone he met. "Isn't there something nice I can do for you?"

People smiled and said, "Yes, indeed, if it wouldn't be too much trouble."

"No trouble at all," said the big elephant. And before long he was helping everybody in town.

He was very good at carrying home lawn mowers and bicycles, baskets of eggs, and any kind of package you could imagine.

The big elephant mowed all the lawns in town in a jiffy, and he pulled the weeds out of everybody's garden.

He was splendid at watering flowers, especially since he didn't need a hose.

That big elephant could shovel coal so fast that he was finished in three winks.

But it took him a long time to carry out the ashes, because the dust blew into his great, enormous, huge, and very tender nose and made him sneeze.

"What I really like best," he said to himself, "is cooking good things to eat."

And he baked an angel cake, high as a mountain and iced with something sweet that tasted like whipped cream and chocolate.

Then he scraped the bowl and everyone had a taste.

When Sunday came, the big elephant took all the children for rides on his shiny, new, and very fast motorcycle.

"Faster!" the children begged.

The big elephant went faster.

"Please beep your horn!" they cried.

Beep! Beep! Beep! went the elephant's big, loud, and very musical horn.

What a fine time those children had!

The big elephant was so popular that he was invited to all the birthday parties. He always accepted with pleasure.

He never forgot to bring a present, and once he was there, he was the life of the party. He played the piano so merrily that in a moment everyone was dancing and singing and having a wonderful time.

"I could play like this forever," the big elephant said happily.

But one day, right in the middle of the fun, CRASH AND BANG! Down went the big heavy piano and the great, enormous, huge, and very heavy elephant and everyone else in the whole party—through the top floor and the main floor—into the cellar!

How exciting! While everyone was helping to clean up . . . the big elephant slipped out. He brought back a whole gallon of strawberry ice cream and the biggest angel cake he had ever made.

There was enough for two helpings all around.

"No more pianos for me!" the big elephant told himself.

He thought he would like to play a big shiny horn all twisted around itself that went Ooompah! Ooompah! Ooompah!

So he went straight to the music store.

He saw drums and fifes and trumpets, and even a big bassoon. But no big shiny horn all twisted around itself. The elephant looked all over town, but there was no such horn to be had.

And soon after that it was winter.

The big elephant got out his great, enormous, huge, and very fancy skates and went ice-skating every day.

Once when he was doing a slow waltz, the children told him about Santa Claus.

"What wonderful news!" he cried.

He hurried home and wrote a neat letter.

"Please bring me a new cap," it said, "and four warm boots, and especially and most of all a big shiny horn such as is not to be had in town."

Then he sat down to think.

He thought perhaps he was not a good enough elephant to get such a present as that.

And he thought, "Perhaps Santa Claus doesn't come to elephants!"

But when he woke up Christmas morning, his stocking was filled with four warm boots and a new red cap. And under it stood the great golden horn, all twisted around itself and shiny as a star!

The big elephant admired the soft fur on his boots. He put on his fine cap. Then he reached out and picked up that wonderful, shiny new horn.

He blew on it once, and out came a lovely note, as shiny and golden as the horn itself.

184

"There's nothing else in the whole world I could wish for," he whispered happily.

All winter long the big elephant played his new horn whenever he had a moment to spare.

He played old tunes and new tunes, and funny little tunes he made up himself.

"He can play every tune we ever heard of!" the people said. "We must ask him to join our town band!"

And in the Fourth of July parade the great, enormous, huge, and very big elephant was right out in front. The flags waved and the crowd cheered as he marched proudly along, playing his shiny horn in the happiest kind of way.

And he was greatly, enormously, hugely, and very, very happy ever after.

What's Up in the Attic?

By Liza Alexander
Illustrated by Tom Cooke

It was a drizzly gray day on Sesame Street. Ernie listened to the dreary sound of the rain against the window. "There's nothing to do!" he groaned.

"Cheer up, Ern!" said Bert. "How about a game of Duckie Land? It used to be our favorite! Come on! Let's go up to the attic and find it!"

Bert gave Ernie a flashlight, and they climbed up the steep stairs to the attic door.

"Ho, hum," sighed Ernie. From the window at the top of the landing he watched the swollen rain clouds scuttle across the sky.

The windows let some light into the gloomy attic. Bert found a couple of old-fashioned lamps and turned them on.

Ernie shined his flashlight around the musty attic. "Wow!" he said, cheering up. "There's lots of great junk up here! Where's Oscar when we need him? Hee, hee!"

"Ernie," said Bert, "this is not junk. The stuff in this attic is like a scrapbook. It can tell us about our past."

Ernie knelt down beside a big old trunk. "Look at this, Bert. It's Great-Aunt Ernestine's trunk. It's been everywhere! Here's a sticker of the Eiffel Tower. That's in Paris, France. And here's a sticker showing the Golden Gate Bridge. That means it's from San Francisco."

"Wouldn't you like to travel and see the world when you grow up?" Bert asked Ernie. "I would."

Bert pulled a fringed jacket out of the trunk. "This trunk is full of family things. This frontier jacket belonged to my grandfather's

187

grandfather, old Mountain Mike. They say he once wrestled a bear to the ground with his bare hands. He had a coonskin cap, too! Let's look for it!"

"Okay, Bert," said Ernie. "A coonskin cap would be pretty neat. We could use it to play cowboy."

"And it would remind us of the old days," said Bert. "I'd look pretty sharp in a coonskin cap. Yessirree! Now, where is it?"

Ernie climbed up on a chair to poke around on top of a wardrobe. Lots of boxes were up there.

Bert dug down deeper into the trunk. "Oh, look what I found, Ernie!" cried Bert. "Uncle Bart's antique paper-clip collection."

"Uh, what's an antique, old buddy?" asked Ernie.

"It's something very old. Some antiques are special because they are different from what we use today, and some are special because they belonged to someone important. Good old Uncle Bart! He gave me my very first paper clip."

Ernie and Bert forgot all about looking for Duckie Land. They even forgot about the rain. But Bert did not forget about the coonskin cap. "It's got to be here somewhere!" said Bert.

Searching in a far corner, Ernie brushed aside some cobwebs
and found his old tricycle. It was much too tiny for him now.

"My, how I've grown!" said Ernie, his knees all scrunched up as
he pedaled his trike. "Let's see how fast this baby can go!"

"Stop it, Ernie!" yelled Bert as Ernie crashed around the attic at
high speed. He knocked past the wardrobe, and some of the
hatboxes tumbled to the floor.

Ernie screeched to a halt in front of a dressmaker's dummy. Bert
wiped his brow. "Phew!" he said.

Then Bert discovered an old-fashioned record player called a
Victrola. He put a record on it and cranked it up to make it go.

Nearby, Ernie found a fancy black jacket and a top hat, and he
put them on. "May I have this dance?" he asked the dummy. They
waltzed around and around to the Victrola's tinny music as Bert
snapped his fingers to the beat.

"Look," said Bert. "It's Dandy the Rocking Horse. Remember
what fun we had riding her when we were little?"

Bert put on Mountain Mike's jacket. He jumped into Dandy's saddle and began to sing, "Home, home on the range . . . where the deer and the antelope play . . .

"Shucks," said Bert. "I sure wish I had that coonskin cap."

Ernie slung an old brown rug over his shoulders and lumbered up behind Bert. "Grrrrrrrr," he said. "I am a bear. Dare you to wrestle me to the ground like old Mountain Mike!"

"Don't be ridiculous," said Bert as he swung down off Dandy. "We've got to find that coonskin cap!"

Then Bert found something interesting. "Oh, my goodness! Here is one of Bernice's baby pigeon feathers. I forgot I saved it. And here is her baby picture. Wasn't she an adorable chick?"

"All right! Look at this!" said Ernie. "My old marbles." He gathered the marbles and looked around for something to put them in.

Then Ernie spotted a furry tail amid the boxes. It was attached to Mountain Mike's coonskin cap!

"Bert will be so happy!" Ernie said to himself as he tossed the marbles into the cap.

Bert was so busy searching that he didn't notice what Ernie was doing.

"The coonskin cap isn't here anymore," he said with a sigh,

190

taking a last look around the attic. "Let's go back downstairs. The sun is coming out anyway."

Ernie balanced all his family treasures in the tricycle basket and rode over to Bert. Ernie plopped the cap on his head, and the marbles from the hat clattered all over the floor.

"Ernie!" said Bert. "You've lost your . . . Hey, you found it! Mountain Mike's coonskin cap!"

"Sure, Bert. Just for you!" said Ernie, and he gave Bert the cap.

"Ernie, what are you planning to do with all this junk?" asked Bert.

"This stuff is just what our place needs," said Ernie. "A dressmaker's dummy, a tiny tricycle, a top hat, and a fuzzy brown rug. Help me carry a few little things, Bert!"

So they carried all their attic discoveries down the stairs.

"This afternoon up in the attic was fun," said Ernie to Bert. "I'm glad I thought of it."

Mister Dog
The Dog Who Belonged to Himself

By Margaret Wise Brown
Illustrated by Garth Williams

Once upon a time there was a funny dog named Crispin's Crispian. He was named Crispin's Crispian because—he belonged to himself.

In the mornings, he woke himself up and he went to the icebox and gave himself some bread and milk. He was a funny old dog. He liked strawberries.

192

Then he took himself for a walk. And he went wherever he wanted to go.

But one morning he didn't know where he wanted to go.

"Just walk and sooner or later you'll get somewhere," he said to himself.

Soon he came to a country where there were lots of dogs. They barked at him and he barked back. Then they all played together.

But he still wanted to go somewhere, so he walked on until he came to a country where there were lots of cats and rabbits.

The cats and rabbits jumped in the air and ran. So Crispian jumped in the air and ran after them.

He didn't catch them because he ran bang into a little boy.

"Who are you and who do you belong to?" asked the little boy.

"I am Crispin's Crispian and I belong to myself," said Crispian. "Who and what are you?"

"I am a boy," said the boy, "and I belong to myself."

"I am so glad," said Crispin's Crispian. "Come and live with me."

Then they went to a butcher shop—"to get his poor dog a bone," Crispian said.

Now, since Crispin's Crispian belonged to himself, he gave himself the bone and trotted home with it.

And the boy's little boy bought a big lamb chop and a bright green vegetable and trotted home with Crispin's Crispian.

Crispin's Crispian lived in a two-story doghouse in a garden. And in his two-story doghouse, he had a little fur living room with a warm fire that crackled all winter and went out in the summer.

His house was always warm. His house had a chimney for the smoke to go out. And upstairs there was a little bedroom with a bed in it and a place for his leash and a pillow under which he hid his bones.

And there was plenty of room in his house for the boy to live there with him.

Crispian had a little kitchen upstairs in his two-story doghouse where he fixed himself a good dinner three times a day because he liked to eat. He liked steaks and chops and roast beef and chopped meat and raw eggs.

This evening he made a bone soup with lots of meat in it. He gave some to the boy, and the boy liked it. The boy didn't give Crispian his chop bone, but he put some of his bright green vegetable in the soup.

And what did Crispian do with his dinner?

Did he put it in his stomach?

Yes, indeed.

He chewed it up and swallowed it into his little fat stomach.

And what did the little boy do with his dinner?

Did he put it in his stomach?

Yes, indeed.

He chewed it up and swallowed it into his little fat stomach.

Crispin's Crispian was a *conservative.* He liked everything at the right time—

dinner at dinnertime,

lunch at lunchtime,

breakfast in time for breakfast,
and sunrise at sunrise,
and sunset at sunset.
And at bedtime—
At bedtime, he liked everything in its own place—
the cup in the saucer,
the chair under the table,
the stars in the heavens,
the moon in the sky,
and himself in his own little bed.
And then what did he do?

Then he curled in a warm little heap and went to sleep. And he dreamed his own dreams.

That was what the dog who belonged to himself did.

And what did the little boy who belonged to himself do?

The boy who belonged to himself curled in a warm little heap and went to sleep. And he dreamed his own dreams.

That was what the boy who belonged to himself did.
GOOD NIGHT AND SWEET DREAMS.

198

My Little Golden Book of Cars and Trucks

By Chari Sue

Illustrated by Richard and Trish Courtney

Kenny loved playing with his car and truck collection more than anything in the world. He had a small model of practically every car and truck imaginable. His favorites were the race cars.

One day Kenny's father took him to the car and truck show in town. It was a very special day.

Kenny and his father drove to the show in their family car. It was a station wagon, with plenty of room in the back for the dog and Kenny's toys when the family went on long trips. There was also a car seat for Kenny's younger sister.

Kenny saw lots of cars on the road. Some of them were like the one his family had, but some were small and sporty. Some were very old, and others were long and sleek. There were even cars without tops on them!

The car and truck show was in the county arena. There was so much to see, Kenny didn't know where to look first. "Let's start with cars and trucks that are used in emergencies," said his father.

"Wow! Look at that fire engine," exclaimed Kenny as they began their tour. It was a big red truck that carried ladders and hoses to help fire fighters put out fires. Kenny was allowed to climb on board and wear the fire chief's hat.

Next was the ambulance. It had a loud siren to help it get through traffic in a hurry. "Many times a police car will go with the ambulance to the hospital," Kenny's father explained.

In the next area, Kenny saw cars and trucks that are used on farms. A man and a woman dressed in cowboy hats and boots explained how the different vehicles are used.

"The plow is used in the fields to turn up the soil. The combine harvester cuts, separates, and cleans the grain while moving over the field," said the woman.

"The forklift can be used to lift hay up to the barn," said the man. "And most farmers drive pickup trucks because they can carry grain, vegetables, and lots of other things."

"Can we go and look at those buses?" Kenny asked as he and his father walked on.

"Sure," his father answered. "That section has all the different vehicles that carry people from place to place."

Kenny recognized the big yellow school bus and the modern city bus. There was even a double-decker bus, and a yellow taxi. But Kenny was most interested in the green and brown vehicles.

"The jeep, the tank, and the canvas-covered truck are all used by the army to transport soldiers," explained his father. Kenny ran off to sit in the jeep.

"Let's check out the cars and trucks that are used to build our roads," called Kenny's father.

Kenny had a lot of these work machines in his toy collection. His favorites were the bulldozer and the ditchdigger, which rip up roads in need of repair.

There was also a dump truck, a cement mixer, and an asphalt spreader, which are used to make new roads when the old ones are torn up.

"Watching the cement mixer go round and round can sure make you dizzy," said Kenny.

At the mobile home area Kenny asked, "Dad, does our house have wheels hidden underneath it? We could take it for a ride sometime!"

"No, I'm afraid not," his father answered with a chuckle. "These trailers are special houses that are designed to be on the move. All of the furniture is nailed down so nothing falls when the home is on the road."

The repair truck and van area was one of the show's most popular places. "The cherry picker is used when broken lights or telephone wires need repair. We stand on the platform and the crane lifts us all the way up to the problem area," explained the service person.

As Kenny rode up high in the cherry picker, he saw some of the other repair vehicles. "There's a tow truck for broken cars," said Kenny.

"That's right," said his father. "And that van carries different tools to help fix plumbing systems, or broken boilers, or anything else in need of repair."

Kenny and his father stopped for ice cream before they moved on to the next area.

Kenny didn't know where to look first in the delivery car and truck area. He saw the big freezer truck, which he had in his toy collection at home. But Kenny also loved the long fuel oil tanker and the mail delivery van.

"I have that truck at home, too," said Kenny. He pointed to a truck used for carrying new cars to the dealers. "I can pile eight toy cars on it.

"I'm having a great time," added Kenny. "And we haven't even gotten to the race cars yet!"

"Well, let's go," said his father.

On the way they had to pass through the service truck area.

"There's the sanitation truck, which picks up garbage, and the snowplow, which clears the roads after a snowstorm, and the street cleaner, which sprays water," Kenny said.

When Kenny looked into the next area, he jumped with excitement.

"Come on," he shouted. "It's the racing cars!"

There were red cars and white cars and blue cars and cars with pinstripes on them. And they could all go very, very fast.

"Can I try on your helmet?" Kenny asked the man at the booth.

"You can have your own helmet," the man said, handing Kenny a shiny blue-and-white sample. "You can even sit behind the wheel," he added as he placed Kenny in the driver's seat.

"Vroom, vroom!" said Kenny.

"That was the best day ever," Kenny told his father that night at bedtime. "I learned so much about different cars and trucks, and I love my new helmet!"

"I can see," said Kenny's father, laughing.

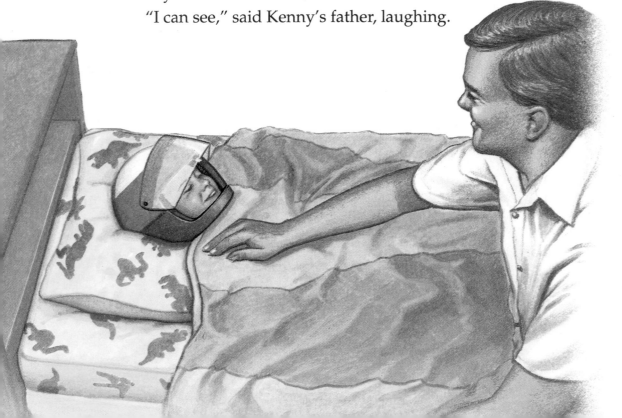

Puss in Boots

By Charles Perrault
Adapted by Eric Suben
Illustrated by Lucinda McQueen

Once there was a poor miller who had three children. When the time came to divide his wealth among them, he had nothing to give but a mill, a donkey, and a cat. The eldest child got the mill, the second child got the donkey, and the youngest child got the cat.

"What good is a cat?" the youngest moaned. "With nothing more than this, I am sure to die of hunger!"

Puss heard these words. "Don't worry, master," he said. "Just give me a sack and a pair of boots, and you will see that things are not so bad as you think."

The master knew that Puss was clever, for he had seen the cat's wonderful ways of catching rats and mice. So he thought the cat might really be able to help him.

When Puss had the things he had asked for, he put on the boots and slung the sack over his shoulder.

He went along till he came to a thicket that was full of rabbits. He put some greens in his sack, then lay still and waited. Soon one of the rabbits sniffed the sack and hopped inside.

Puss quickly pulled the sack shut.

He went to the palace and asked to speak to the king. "Here, sire," he said, "is a rabbit that the Marquis of Carabas asked me to present to you."

"Tell your master," replied the king, "that I thank him."

206

The next day Puss hid in a wheat field and held his sack open. He caught two partridges and went to present them to the king. The king received the partridges with pleasure.

Every day for the next few months Puss brought the king some small game for his supper.

One day, when he was at the palace, Puss learned that the king was going for a drive along the river with his daughter, the most beautiful princess in the world.

Puss ran home and said to his master, "If you follow my advice, your fortune will be made: You must bathe in the river at the place that I show you. Then let me do what I will."

The master did what the cat advised him, though he didn't know what good might come of it.

While the young man was bathing, the king and his daughter happened to pass by. Puss began to cry with all his might, "Help, help! The Marquis of Carabas is drowning!"

When he heard this cry, the king looked out of the carriage. After recognizing the cat who had brought him so much tasty game, he ordered his guards to go quickly to the aid of the Marquis of Carabas.

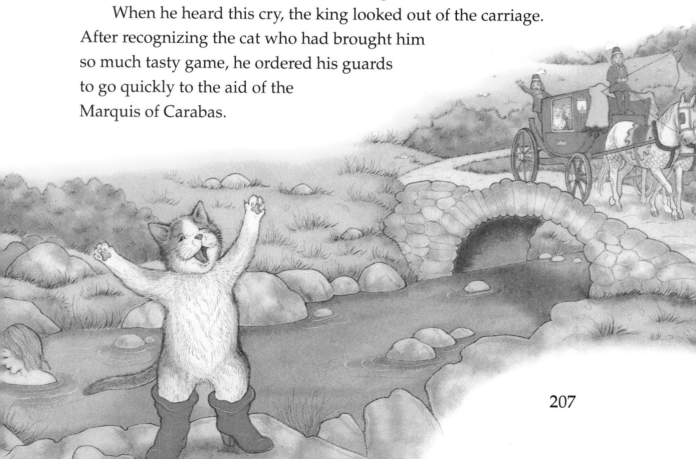

207

Meanwhile, Puss told the king that some robbers had stolen his master's fine clothes and thrown the young man into the river. But really Puss himself had hidden his master's rags under a rock.

The king at once ordered the guards to fetch one of his handsomest suits from the palace.

Puss's master was a good-looking youth. When the beautiful princess saw how fine he looked in her father's rich clothes, she instantly fell in love with him.

208

The king asked the marquis to step into the carriage and ride with them.

Puss, delighted that his plan was beginning to succeed, ran on ahead. When he came upon some peasants who were harvesting wheat, he said, "Good harvesters, tell the king that this wheat belongs to the Marquis of Carabas, or you will all be punished severely."

Sure enough, when the king passed, he asked the harvesters, "Whose field is this?"

"It belongs to the Marquis of Carabas," they all said together.

"You have fine fields here, Marquis," said the king.

Puss kept running ahead of the carriage. Wherever he saw people working in the fields, he made the same threat. And wherever the king stopped to ask the name of the landlord, he heard the same answer.

"I never knew of anyone who owned as much fine farmland as you," the king told the marquis.

Now, all that fine farmland really belonged to a rich ogre. Puss was careful to find out about the ogre and the things he did.

Puss finally arrived at the ogre's handsome castle and demanded to speak to the owner.

The ogre received Puss as politely as an ogre could and asked him to sit down.

"They tell me," said Puss, "that you are able to change yourself into any big animal—for example, a lion or an elephant."

"That is true," the ogre said. "And to prove it to you, I will become a lion."

Puss was so frightened to see a lion before him that he raced up the wall and clung to the rafters.

210

When the ogre had returned to his original form, Puss came down and spoke again.

"They tell me, too," said Puss, "that you are able to take the form of the smallest animal—for example, a rat or a mouse. I cannot believe that!"

"You will see," replied the ogre. And he changed himself into a mouse that scurried across the floor.

Before another moment had passed, Puss pounced and ate the mouse.

Just then Puss heard the king's carriage passing over the castle drawbridge. He ran out and said to the king, "Your Majesty, welcome to the castle of the Marquis of Carabas!"

"What? Marquis!" cried the king. "This handsome castle is yours, too! Let us see inside, if you please."

The marquis offered his hand to the young princess, and they all went inside. There they found a magnificent feast waiting to be eaten. It was the ogre's leftover lunch.

The king was thoroughly pleased with the meal and with the wealthy Marquis of Carabas. He said, "I will have no one but you for my son-in-law."

The marquis, bowing deeply, accepted the honor and married the princess that same day. Puss became a great lord and chased mice only for fun forever after.

Ariel's Underwater Adventure

Adapted by Michael Teitelbaum
Illustrated by Ron Dias

Once upon a time there was a beautiful little mermaid named Ariel. She was the youngest daughter of the Sea King, Triton. Even though she lived at the bottom of the ocean, Ariel was not interested in her watery world. This little princess was only interested in the world above the ocean—the world of humans.

Ariel spent most of her time searching through sunken ships, looking for objects that had once belonged to humans. To Ariel these rusty old things were wonderful treasures.

One afternoon Ariel was treasure hunting in a graveyard of old sunken ships with her best friend, Flounder the fish.

"Come on, Flounder!" shouted Ariel as she swam into a broken-down ship. "Let's look in here."

"Are you sure it's safe?" asked Flounder.

"Sure," answered Ariel. "Follow me."

Inside, Ariel found a chest full of treasures.

"Oh, Flounder!" gasped Ariel. "Have you ever seen anything this wonderful in your entire life?"

Among the objects in the ship, Ariel found a fork and a pipe. "This is great!" the little mermaid cried. She put the objects into a pouch. "I don't have any of these in my collection yet!"

Just then Flounder heard a noise. "W-what was that?" he cried.

"I didn't hear anything," said Ariel, who was too busy looking for more treasures to notice any strange sounds.

Trembling with fear, Flounder peeked outside the doorway of the ship. There, with his huge mouthful of sharp teeth open wide, was a shark.

"Shark!" screamed Flounder as he raced back inside.

Ariel grabbed her bag of treasures. She and Flounder swam

quickly to the upper deck. The shark followed, snapping his jaws. Ariel and Flounder squeezed through a porthole.

The small porthole didn't stop the shark. He crashed right through the side of the ship after them.

The mermaid and her little companion were swimming hard, but they were barely staying ahead of the shark's terrible jaws. The shark lunged at them, his jaws snapping the ship's mast as if it were a matchstick.

The two swam as fast as they could toward a huge old anchor. The shark followed, only inches behind them.

"I hope this works," gasped Ariel.

"M-me too," cried Flounder.

When they reached the anchor, Ariel and Flounder slipped through the ring at the top. The shark tried to follow, but he was too big. His enormous face got stuck in the anchor.

"Let's get out of here," said Ariel. "We can head up to the surface to show Scuttle my new treasures."

On the surface Ariel and Flounder visited with their friend Scuttle the sea gull. Ariel pulled one of her new treasures out of the pouch.

"Do you know what this is?" Ariel asked Scuttle, handing him the fork.

"Why, certainly," replied the cockeyed sea gull. "After all, I'm the world's greatest expert on humans. This is a . . . dinglehopper. Humans use it to straighten their hair, like this." Scuttle ran the old fork through Ariel's hair.

"What's this, Scuttle?" asked Ariel, this time handing him the pipe.

"This is most definitely a . . . a snarfblatt!" he answered. "It's used to make music." Scuttle blew into the pipe, but nothing came out except water. "Hmm. Nothing worse than a defective snarfblatt!"

Soon it was time for Ariel and Flounder to leave. They said good-bye to Scuttle and returned to the undersea kingdom.

Ariel went to her secret cave, where she hid all her human treasures.

The two friends were playing with Ariel's special collection when suddenly the cave got very dark. Ariel looked up through an opening and noticed something on the surface of the water blocking out the moonlight.

"I'm going to see what that is, Flounder," said Ariel.

On the ocean's surface was a very big ship.

"How beautiful it is!" exclaimed Ariel. "We've got to get a closer look."

Ariel reached up and peered over the side of the ship while Flounder looked on from the water below. Ariel saw a young man. His shipmates were singing and dancing.

"I've never seen a human this close before," said Ariel to Scuttle, who was also curious about the humans and had come for a better look.

"He's very handsome, isn't he?" said Ariel, looking at the young man the sailors called Prince Eric.

"He looks kind of hairy to me," said Scuttle, looking at Prince Eric's sheepdog, Max.

But Ariel didn't hear the sea gull. All she could think about was the young man—the one she would someday join in the world of humans. Ariel was falling in love.

Suddenly, without warning, a big storm came up. Rain poured down, lightning flashed, and the wind tossed the ship like a toy sailboat. Ariel watched Prince Eric as he and his crew tried to keep the ship afloat.

As the ship tossed and turned in the water, a bolt of lightning hit the mast. The burning mast collapsed onto a keg of gunpowder. The explosion threw Prince Eric overboard into the raging waves.

"The prince!" shouted Ariel.

Prince Eric sank under the water. Ariel knew that if she didn't act at once, her handsome prince would drown.

Ariel dived into the sea. She grabbed Prince Eric and brought him up to the surface. Holding him tightly, she swam to shore and dragged the prince onto the sandy beach.

216

While the prince lay sleeping, Ariel stroked his hair and sang him a beautiful love song. How Ariel wished she could be with Prince Eric in the human world!

Before the prince began to stir, Ariel heard his crew coming. She knew she had to leave before she was seen by the humans.

Blowing the prince a kiss, Ariel turned and dived back into the ocean.

Ariel and Flounder returned to her secret cave so the little mermaid could be with her human treasures.

"Oh, Flounder," said Ariel. "Prince Eric's so handsome. I can hardly wait until I see him again."

Flounder just smiled. Ariel combed her hair with her dinglehopper and wished for the day when she would be with her human prince forever.

The Nutcracker

Retold by Rita Balducci
Illustrated by Barbara Lanza

Once there was a little girl named Clara whose family was having a wonderful party on Christmas Eve. There was a beautiful Christmas tree and lots of delicious food. Clara ran back and forth to the front door to welcome the guests.

"Merry Christmas!" she said as each one kissed her on the cheek. Then they all went inside to dance and eat and open their Christmas presents.

The last to arrive was Clara's godfather, Herr Drosselmeyer. All the children loved him very much because he was such a wonderful storyteller. Clara thought he could even perform magic!

"Merry Christmas, Clara," he said, handing her a heavy package.

"Merry Christmas—and thank you!" Clara cried, lifting a large wooden nutcracker from the wrappings. "He looks like a very brave soldier," she said.

"And so he is," Herr Drosselmeyer replied.

Just then the musicians began to play a lively tune, and the grown-ups joined together to dance.

Clara carried her nutcracker over to where her cousins and friends were all playing with their new dolls. She held him very carefully and hummed a soft Christmas carol. All of a sudden Clara's little brother, Fritz, jumped up from behind the sofa and grabbed the nutcracker away from his sister.

"No, Fritz, no!" Clara cried, chasing him. Soon all the children were running after Fritz. But the nutcracker was very heavy, and Fritz was a very little boy. The nutcracker crashed to the floor and broke.

Sadly Clara picked up her injured nutcracker and showed him to Herr Drosselmeyer.

"Why, Clara," he said, tying his handkerchief around the nutcracker's broken jaw, "many good soldiers get hurt in battle. This will be his bandage, and you will be his nurse." And he wiped her tears away and handed the nutcracker back to her.

Clara was a very good little nurse. She gently tucked the nutcracker into the doll's bed she had received as a Christmas present. She stayed by his side until all the guests had gone home.

Then she kissed him good night and went up to bed.

But Clara could not stop thinking about her nutcracker. So back downstairs she crept and lifted him from the little bed. Then she curled up on the sofa and fell asleep with the nutcracker in her arms.

While Clara was sleeping, Herr Drosselmeyer came into the room. He quietly took the handkerchief off the nutcracker's jaw and gently waved it over Clara and the nutcracker. Suddenly the nutcracker changed into a handsome prince, standing guard over Clara while she slept.

Later that night Clara woke up. "Oh, my goodness!" she cried, for tremendous mice were running all over the room. Then she saw her nutcracker, who was now a handsome prince. He was bravely fighting a mouse that was wearing a crown on its head.

"Leave him alone!" Clara shouted at the wicked mouse. She jumped off the sofa and pulled the mouse's long tail. The mouse became so frightened that it ran away, with all the other mice squeaking after it.

"Thank you for your help," said the prince, picking up the crown,

220

which had fallen from the mouse's head. "I would like to invite you to the Land of Sweets so all my friends can thank you, too."

The prince placed the crown upon Clara's head, and her nightgown became a beautiful dress that sparkled and shimmered.

Together they stepped outside. The falling snow whisked around them in a pretty white dance, carrying them to the Land of Sweets.

Everyone living in the Land of Sweets was named after delicious things to eat. When the prince and Clara arrived, he told his friends all about the battle with the huge mice and how Clara had saved him.

"Hurray for Clara!" they all shouted. Then they carried Clara and the prince over to two beautiful candy-cane chairs.

The people of the Land of Sweets performed beautiful dances for Clara and the prince.

The first to perform were candy canes wearing red stripes. Then a dainty Sugar Plum Fairy danced with a soldier.

The Dew Drop Fairy gracefully twirled before them, followed by many little angels with tiny wings. Even the flowers danced in the Land of Sweets, waving their pretty petals.

Clara's favorite dancer was Mother Ginger. She wore a big wide skirt, and underneath it were six little children. They raced out and took each other's hands, dancing together in a circle, laughing and skipping. When their turn was over, they scrambled back under Mother Ginger's wide skirt.

When all the dancers were finished, Clara and the prince stood up and clapped and clapped.

"I think it is time for us to go," the prince said. "But we will come back to the Land of Sweets every Christmas Eve from now on."

And then he called for his sleigh, which was drawn by two reindeer. After waving good-bye to their friends, Clara and the prince flew off together into the early morning sky, home to a very merry Christmas!

222

Tiny Dinosaurs

By Steven Lindblom
Illustrated by Gino D'Achille

Paul C. Sereno, Consultant
Assistant Professor, University of Chicago

Millions of years ago huge dinosaurs walked the earth. They were the biggest animals that ever lived on land.

Ultrasaurus (ul-tra-SAWR-us) may have been bigger than a five-story building.

Fierce *Tyrannosaurus* (tye-ran-o-SAWR-us) was as tall as a telephone pole and weighed as much as a school bus. When he ran, the ground must have trembled.

Hiding in the bushes as these monsters thundered by were other, smaller creatures. What were these creatures? Some were lizards, others were small mammals, and others were . . . TINY DINOSAURS!

Not all dinosaurs were giants. Dinosaurs came in all sizes, just as animals do today. Many dinosaurs were no bigger than you. Some were even smaller.

Dinosaurs once lived all over the world. Some may have lived right where you live today. But the world did not look like it does now. There were no people, houses, or roads then. Many kinds of strange plants grew everywhere. The weather may have been much warmer than it is now.

Saltopus (sal-TOE-pus) was one of the earliest and tiniest dinosaurs. It lived 160 million years ago. *Saltopus* was only the size of a cat and ate bugs and lizards. With its long legs it looked like a featherless roadrunner and must have been very fast.

People used to think of dinosaurs as being great big lizards, but we now know that they were not. Lizards are cold-blooded, and today scientists think some dinosaurs may have been warm-blooded. Many dinosaurs walked on their hind legs, like birds. They carried their tails in the air for balance instead of dragging them on the ground. Lizards cannot do those things.

Compsognathus (comp-so-NATH-us) was a very small dinosaur. It had a close cousin, *Archaeopteryx* (ar-kee-OP-ter-ix). Both had long tails and sharp teeth. Looking at the bones of these two cousins, it is very hard to tell them apart.

But *Archaeopteryx* also had wings and feathers. It was a good flier. It may also have been able to climb trees, using the claws on its wings and legs.

These tiny dinosaurs fed on insects, lizards, and other tiny animals. They were fast and agile. They had to keep out of the way of their hungry bigger cousins.

Being such little animals in a world of giants must have made

Compsognathus

Archaeopteryx

Deinonychus

most of the tiny dinosaurs very timid. They probably lived like mice or chipmunks do today, darting about quietly in search of food.

Not *Deinonychus* (dine-o-NYE-kus), though. A little smaller than a man, it was one of the fiercest dinosaurs of all. *Deinonychus* had a mouth full of sharp teeth, and a sharp middle claw on each back foot for slashing. It was very fast and could outrun anything it couldn't eat.

But not all the tiny dinosaurs were meat-eaters. Some ate only plants. *Psittacosaurus* (sit-a-ko-SAWR-us), or "parrot-lizard," had a powerful beak like a parrot's. It used its beak to eat tough plants and small trees, which it ground up in its stomach with stones it swallowed.

Another plant-eater, *Ammosaurus* (am-mo-SAWR-us), was only the size of a large dog. Like its big cousin *Apatosaurus* (a-pat-o-SAWR-us), it spent most of its time on four legs, although it could stand and walk on two.

Heterodontosaurus

Heterodontosaurus (het-er-o-don-to-SAWR-us) was only the size of a turkey and fed on plants. With its grinding teeth it could eat almost anything. With its biting teeth it could fight off other dinosaurs.

Another tiny dinosaur, *Scutellosaurus* (scut-tle-o-SAWR-us), didn't need sharp teeth to protect itself. Its back was covered with bony armor plates. *Scutellosaurus* had a tail that was twice as long as its body.

Some tiny dinosaurs were tiny because they were babies. Even the biggest of the dinosaurs were tiny when they hatched from eggs.

Scutellosaurus

Apatosaurus

Many dinosaur babies were so small, they would have fit in your hand. Even a newly hatched *Apatosaurus* was probably smaller than a cat.

You might not recognize a baby *Stegosaurus* (steg-o-SAWR-us) unless you saw it with a grown-up one. *Stegosauruses* may not have grown their back plates until they got older.

Maiasaura (mye-a-SAWR-a) was only the size of a robin when it hatched from its egg, but it grew up to be 30 feet long.

How did such big dinosaur mothers ever care for such tiny babies? They must have been very gentle for their size. Scientists

Stegosaurus

used to think that dinosaurs just laid their eggs and left them, the way turtles do today. Now we believe that many dinosaurs fed and cared for their young, the way birds do.

A dinosaur mother was too big to sit on her eggs without breaking them. Instead she covered them with leaves and moss to keep them warm until they hatched.

The little dinosaurs would stay close to the nest until they were big enough to go off on their own.

Many dinosaurs lived in herds with other dinosaurs like themselves. There would have been many little dinosaurs in the group at one time. Did they play with each other? Maybe they did, chasing each other and splashing about in the water.

The last dinosaurs died out 65 million years ago. You can never see live dinosaurs—just their bones. But many scientists think today's birds are direct relatives of the dinosaurs. So the next time you feed the birds, you can imagine you are feeding tiny dinosaurs!

Maiasaura

Bugs Bunny
Stowaway

Written by Justine Korman

One day Bugs Bunny was strolling along the docks not far from his rabbit hole. There he had a beautiful view of boats coming and going on the ocean.

Suddenly Bugs saw a sight even more beautiful—a big crate of carrots! Bugs opened the crate and ate and ate until his teeth were tired. Then he crawled inside and fell asleep.

When he woke up, Bugs felt the ocean rocking beneath him and smelled the salty sea air.

"Where am I?" Bugs wondered. He looked out one porthole, then another, and realized that he was on a ship in the middle of the ocean.

"I hope this ship's going to Pismo Beach," Bugs thought. "I could use a vacation."

Bugs Bunny went up to the main deck and saw Captain Yosemite Sam steering his pirate ship while studying a handwritten map.

Bugs tapped Sam on the shoulder and asked, "What's up, doc?"

"What're ya doin' here, ya long-eared landlubber?!" Sam shrieked. "Are ya tryin' ta steal muh treasure?"

"What treasure?" Bugs asked innocently.

Sam grabbed the map.

"Look, doc, I'm not interested in treasure," Bugs began. "Just drop me off at Pismo Beach. On the way, I'll help with the ship. You look like you could use a crew."

Sam decided he might as well put Bugs Bunny to work.

"The first thing I want you to do is check the lifeboats," Captain Sam said. "Make sure they have all the emergency supplies," he added, handing Bugs a list.

While Bugs checked off the supplies in one boat, Sam made small cuts in the ropes holding the boat to his ship. "So long, ya stinkin' stowaway," Sam thought, chuckling.

By the time Bugs reached the end of the list, the lifeboat was hanging by threads.

"It's all here," Bugs reported.

"Then haul 'er up!" Sam commanded, stepping back to avoid the expected splash.

But to Sam's surprise, the ropes didn't break.

"What the—I mean, hmm, I better check the boat myself," Sam said, wondering why the ropes had held.

As soon as Sam stepped into the lifeboat, the ropes broke. The boat fell into the ocean with a great splash.

Bugs leaned over the side of the ship.

"Hey, ya long-eared landlubber!" Sam shrieked. "Throw me a rope!"

"Whatever you say, doc," Bugs replied.

Back on his ship, Sam came up with a fiendish plan. "This'll get that bucktoothed barnacle offa muh ship!" Sam muttered gleefully.

"It's time to clean out the cannon," Sam told Bugs.

Sailor Bugs saluted. "Aye, aye, Cap'n."

"The only way to get it really clean is to crawl inside," Sam said.

"Aye, aye, sir," Bugs Bunny said, scrambling inside the cannon with brushes and rags. He sang while he scrubbed the insides of the dark cannon.

Sam tiptoed to the cannon, struck a match, and thought, "Good-bye, ya carrot-chompin' critter!"

He lit the fuse and plugged his ears.

Sam waited, but nothing happened. Then Bugs scrambled out of the cannon.

"It's all clean, doc," Crewman Bunny reported.

"What in tarnation?" Sam exclaimed. "I mean—hmm, something's wrong. I better check the cannon myself," he said with a frown.

"The dang-blasted thing's supposed to fire," Sam muttered from inside the cannon.

"Maybe you need to release the safety catch," Bugs said, flipping the catch.

"Wait!" Sam yelled,
but it was too late.

BOOM! Sam flew way up
into the sky, where an angry sea
gull squawked in his ear.

"Land ho!" Yosemite Sam yelled as he zoomed over the waves and
landed on the sandy shore of Pirate Island.

By the time Bugs lowered a lifeboat and rowed to the island, Sam
was already searching for the treasure.

"Two paces to the left," he muttered, studying his map.

"What's up, doc?" Bugs asked, leaning over Sam's shoulder.

"Take one more look at muh map and I'll fix you into fricassee!"
Sam blustered.

"Don't mind me. I'm just lookin' for coconuts," Bugs said, strolling
away. To himself he muttered, "Whadda maroon! He's holding that map
upside down. The treasure isn't buried in the valley—it's in a cave near
the top of that volcano."

Bugs climbed the smoking volcano. Near the top he found a cave filled with treasure chests gleaming with pirate gold. "There's enough treasure here to make a gold carrot the size of Mount Rushmore," Bugs said, whistling.

But before he could grab any of the gold, Bugs heard a loud rumble.

Bugs raced for shore as fast as he could. "The volcano's going to blow!" he warned Sam.

Sam shook the map at Bugs. "You can't fool me, ya flea-bitten treasure-napper! The gold's in the cave, and I'mma gonna get it!" Sam hollered as he ran up the rumbling volcano.

Sam reached the cave just as the volcano erupted. "Not again!" yelled Sam as he felt himself being lifted high above the shaking cave.

The explosion sent Sam and the treasure flying through the air. He landed with a thud on the deck of his ship atop a mountain of gold.

Sam grabbed two handfuls of gold coins and threw them over his head in a glittering shower.

"I won, ya mangy critter!" he yelled to Bugs, who was rowing the lifeboat from the shore to the ship.

Bugs just shrugged his shoulders.

Sam wondered what was going on. Wherever he looked the ocean was rising. Then Sam realized his ship was going down! The treasure chests had made holes in his ship!

"Save me! Save the treasure!" Yosemite Sam cried.

"Sure thing," Bugs said when he'd reached the sinking ship. The crate of carrots floated by. He hauled it into the lifeboat.

"Are you out of your carrot-pickin' mind?" Sam screamed.

In a few minutes all the pirate gold was beneath the blue sea, and Sam and Bugs were safe in the lifeboat.

Bugs was relaxing. He slowly munched on a carrot while Sam rowed, brooding over his sunken treasure.

"Ah hates rabbits," Sam grumbled.

"Relax, doc," Bugs said. "It's only two hundred more miles to Pismo Beach."

Rapunzel

Adapted by Marianna Mayer
Illustrated by Sheilah Beckett

There was once a husband and wife who lived near a grand castle. The couple didn't know it, but the castle was owned by a wicked sorceress. Behind the castle wall was a wonderful garden full of beautiful flowers and good things to eat. The wife could look out and see the castle garden from her cottage.

A time came when the husband and wife were going to have their first child. The sorceress, who had no children, decided to cast a spell on the woman. If the spell worked, the sorceress could have the child for herself.

That very day the wife began to long for rapunzel, a blue-flowering plant that grew only in the sorceress's garden.

As time passed, the spell made the wife long for the plant more and more. Finally she began to feel ill and begged her husband to get some rapunzel leaves from the castle garden. She knew that if she ate a salad of the leaves, she would feel better again.

That night the husband climbed over the garden wall and stole some of the fresh green rapunzel leaves. His wife ate them greedily and began to feel better. But the taste only made her want more.

Reluctantly the husband returned night after night. Then one evening, when the moon was full, he slipped over the wall to find the tall, dark figure of the sorceress waiting for him.

"Thief! How dare you steal from me?" she said angrily.

Frightened, the man fell to his knees before her and tried to explain.

When the sorceress heard him speak of the coming of his first child, her manner changed and her voice softened.

"You may have all the rapunzel you wish, on one condition. When the child is born, you must give it to me!"

When the husband refused, the sorceress said, "I'm sure your wife will agree."

To his surprise, the man's wife did agree to give the child up, for the spell was still working. The wife said, "Surely the owner of that beautiful castle is a great lady. She will take good care of our child."

In the next few weeks the wife grew healthier. She was given all the rapunzel she wished, and rapidly her strength returned. Soon a beautiful baby girl was born to her. The baby was named Rapunzel, after the blue-flowering plant her mother loved so much.

As promised, Rapunzel's parents had to give the baby to the sorceress.

When the heartbroken parents left, the sorceress said to herself, laughing, "Now I will have the child all to myself!"

For twelve years she kept Rapunzel in the castle, and the girl grew to be very beautiful. Her eyes were as blue as the blue-flowering plant she was named after, and her long, silken hair was as golden as the sun. The sorceress never allowed Rapunzel's hair to be cut. When it began to trail on the floor, the sorceress made one long braid of it and wound it around Rapunzel's head like a golden crown.

On Rapunzel's twelfth birthday the sorceress moved her to a secluded tower. The tower did not have stairs or a door, but high at the top was a small window.

When the sorceress wanted to visit Rapunzel, she stood beneath the window and called, "Rapunzel! Rapunzel! Let down your golden hair!" The girl uncoiled her long, thick braid and let it fall like a rope from the open window until it reached the sorceress's outstretched hands. The sorceress climbed to the top of the tower and entered the window.

While they were together, the sorceress combed and braided Rapunzel's hair and always asked the same question: "Who have you seen since I was last here?"

Rapunzel always answered, "No one, Stepmother." For who would the poor, lonely girl see while locked up in the tower?

One night a handsome young prince came riding through the forest. He heard Rapunzel's sweet voice as she sang a beautiful song. The prince followed the sound till he came to the tower, but could find no way in. Since it was late, he decided to rest until morning.

At daybreak he was awakened by an old woman's harsh call. "Rapunzel!" the voice demanded. "Rapunzel! Let down your golden hair!"

All at once the golden braid came tumbling down from the open window. When the prince saw the sorceress grab hold of the braid and climb up the tower, he whispered to himself, "So that is how one is to get inside."

Patiently the prince waited, and at last he saw the sorceress leave. Then he decided to try his luck. He called, "Rapunzel! Rapunzel! Let down your golden hair." As soon as she did, he held her long braid and climbed the tower.

Rapunzel and the prince fell in love the moment they saw each other. They wanted to be together, but they had to find a way to get Rapunzel down from the tower. The prince promised to return the next day with a rope ladder. "Then you'll be free at last," he told Rapunzel.

On the following morning, when the sorceress came to visit, she asked, "Who have you seen, Rapunzel, since I was last here?"

Rapunzel couldn't tell a lie, and she told the sorceress all about the handsome prince.

The sorceress flew into a rage and took hold of Rapunzel's braid. She cut the beautiful hair with a pair of scissors—*Snip, snap! Snip, snap!*—and the braid fell to the floor. Then, in an instant, the heartless sorceress carried Rapunzel far off to the most deserted place in the whole world and left her there alone.

At nightfall, when the prince arrived to rescue Rapunzel, he called, "Rapunzel! Rapunzel! Let down your golden hair!" When the braid came falling down from the window, the prince took hold of it and climbed up the tower. But instead of seeing his beloved Rapunzel, he found the cruel sorceress waiting for him.

She fixed her cold black eyes upon him and cast a spell that blinded him. "Rapunzel is lost to you forever," she cried. "You will never see her again!"

The prince fell from the window, and though he escaped with his life, he could no longer see. Lost and alone, he stumbled away to wander hopelessly in search of Rapunzel.

Years passed until at last the unhappy prince came to the most

deserted place in the whole world. All of a sudden he heard a sweet voice singing. Though it had been many years since he had heard the voice, it was familiar. Eagerly he followed the sound, and soon the poor young man stood before Rapunzel.

When she saw her beloved prince, Rapunzel threw her arms around his neck and wept for joy. Her tears fell upon his eyes, and all at once the sorceress's evil spell was broken. The prince could see Rapunzel as well as ever before.

The prince led Rapunzel back to his own kingdom, where they were welcomed with great rejoicing. At last they were free of the wicked sorceress, and they lived out their lives together in love.

Fire Engines to the Rescue

By Janet Campbell

Illustrated by Courtney Studios

With appreciation to the Joplin Fire Department

It is morning in the city—time for roll call at Fire Company Number 2.

Ten fire fighters line up outside the firehouse. The lieutenant calls out their names.

"Here!" says each fire fighter.

The fire fighters from the night shift are going home to get a good day's sleep.

"Good luck," they call to the day-shift fire fighters.

After roll call, the fire fighters check their gear.

They each have a coat that protects them from both water and heat.

241

It is called a turnout coat. They have rubber boots to keep their feet dry. They each have a hard helmet to protect their head from falling objects.

Next the fire fighters inspect the apparatus—the vehicles they use during a fire. They check the gas, the oil, and the tires of the cherry-picker ladder truck, the pumper truck, and the chief's car.

The fire fighters check the controls that work the cherry-picker bucket. They also check the ladders.

There is lots of equipment on the ladder truck. One fire fighter checks the axes. Another checks the hooks attached to long poles. A third fire fighter checks the power saw stored on the truck.

The breathing masks are inspected to make sure the tanks are full of air.

Is Ladder Truck Number 12 ready? Yes!

The pumper truck carries everything the fire fighters need for spraying water on a fire.

The crew checks the hoses to make sure they are not tangled. They test the pump and the pressure gauges. Then they check the breathing masks.

Is Pumper Truck Number 3 ready? Yes!

But there are other kinds of work to do, too.

Upstairs in the firehouse kitchen, one fire fighter takes his turn making lunch. He is cooking soup.

Downstairs, two fire fighters fix some of the small equipment. One puts a new handle on an ax. The other replaces the pole that holds a hook.

Three fire fighters practice first aid.

One fire fighter is on house watch, waiting for a fire signal.

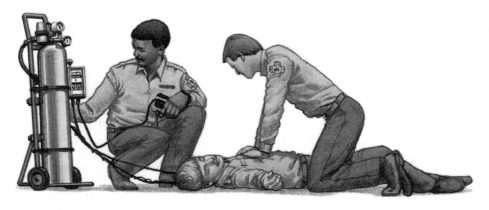

Suddenly a buzzer sounds. A computer printout is coming in from central dispatch.

Fire Company Number 2—fire in progress—Sawyer's apartment complex—Broadway and 12th Streets.

The fire bell rings. Some of the fire fighters come sliding down the shiny brass pole.

All the fire fighters put on their coats and helmets. They step out of their shoes, pull on their big rubber boots, and jump onto the apparatus.

Sirens wail, lights flash, bells clang. The chief's car speeds out of the firehouse. Pumper Truck Number 3 and Ladder Truck Number 12 are right behind it.

At the fire, the chief tells his fire fighters what to do. One fire fighter connects the pumper truck to the hydrant. Then she opens the hydrant with a wrench.

Two other fire fighters unroll the hoses. Another turns on the pump when the hoses are in place.

Swoooosh! Water shoots from the hoses. It takes two fire fighters to hold each wiggly hose. Another fire fighter must stay with the pumper truck.

Ssssssss! The fire hisses with steam.

The crew from Pumper Truck Number 3 is hard at work, trying to put out the fire.

The crew of Ladder Truck Number 12 is busy, too.

One fire fighter pulls down a burning awning with a hook, so it won't fall on anyone.

One fire fighter breaks windows in the burning building with an ax before the heat makes the glass explode.

Another fire fighter cuts a hole in the roof with a power saw to let out smoke.

Look! Two people are trapped on the fire escape. Flames are shooting up from below!

"Get that bucket up there!" shouts the chief.

One fire fighter climbs into the cherry-picker bucket. Up it goes, all the way to the fourth floor.

Another fire fighter climbs down from the roof to help the people into the bucket.

The bucket takes the people safely down to the ground.

Hurray for the brave fire fighters!

The fire fighters give the people oxygen to help them breathe. Then an ambulance comes to take them to the hospital.

The people are going to be all right.

The fire has been put out. Pumper Truck Number 3 and Ladder Truck Number 12 have returned to the firehouse.

First the tired fire fighters clean the apparatus. Then they put their gear away.

Next the fire fighters go to their lockers and put on clean, dry clothes.

It is way past lunchtime, but the cook still has to feed the hungry fire fighters.

"Soup's on!" he shouts to the ones who still haven't come upstairs.

And the fire fighters eat up every last spoonful.

Tawny Scrawny Lion

By Kathryn Jackson
Illustrated by Gustaf Tenggren

Once there was a tawny, scrawny, hungry lion who never could get enough to eat.

He chased monkeys on Monday—kangaroos on Tuesday—zebras on Wednesday—bears on Thursday—camels on Friday—and on Saturday, elephants!

And since he caught everything he ran after, that lion should have been as fat as butter. But he wasn't at all. The more he ate, the scrawnier and hungrier he grew.

The other animals didn't feel one bit safe. They stood at a distance and tried to talk things over with the tawny, scrawny lion.

"It's all your fault for running away," he grumbled. "If I didn't have to run, run, run for every single bite I get, I'd be fat as butter and sleek as satin. Then I wouldn't have to eat so much, and you'd last longer!"

Just then, a fat little rabbit came hopping through the forest, picking berries. All the big animals looked at him and grinned slyly.

"Rabbit," they said. "Oh, you lucky rabbit! We appoint you to talk things over with the lion."

That made the little rabbit feel very proud.

"What shall I talk about?" he asked eagerly.

"Any old thing," said the big animals. "The important thing is to go right up close."

So the fat little rabbit hopped right up to the big hungry lion and counted his ribs.

"You look much too scrawny to talk things over," he said. "So how about supper at my house first?"

"What's for supper?" asked the lion.

The little rabbit said, "Carrot stew." That sounded awful to the lion. But the little rabbit said, "Yes, sir, my five fat sisters and my four fat brothers are making a delicious big carrot stew right now!"

"What are we waiting for?" cried the lion. And he went hopping away with the little rabbit, thinking of ten fat rabbits and looking just as jolly as you please.

"Well," grinned all the big animals. "That should take care of Tawny Scrawny for today."

Before very long, the lion began to wonder if they would ever get to the rabbit's house.

First, the fat little rabbit kept stopping to pick berries and mushrooms and all sorts of good-smelling herbs. And when his basket was full, what did he do but flop down on the riverbank!

"Wait a bit," he said. "I want to catch a few fish for the stew."

That was almost too much for the hungry lion.

For a moment, he thought he would have to eat that one little rabbit then and there. But he kept saying "Five fat sisters and four fat brothers" over and over to himself. And at last the two were on their way again.

"Here we are!" said the rabbit, hopping around a turn with the lion close behind him. Sure enough, there was the rabbit's house, with a big pot of carrot stew bubbling over an open fire.

And sure enough, there were nine more fat, merry little rabbits hopping around it!

When they saw the fish, they popped them into the stew, along with the mushrooms and herbs. The stew began to smell very good indeed.

And when they saw the tawny, scrawny lion, they gave him a big bowl of hot stew. And then they hopped about so busily that, really, it would have been quite a job for that tired, hungry lion to catch even one of them!

So he gobbled his stew, but the rabbits filled his bowl again. When he had eaten all he could hold, they heaped his bowl with berries.

And when the berries were gone—the tawny, scrawny lion wasn't scrawny anymore! He felt so good and fat and comfortable that he couldn't even move.

"Here's a fine thing!" he said to himself. "All these fat little rabbits, and I haven't room inside for even one!"

He looked at all those fine, fat little rabbits and wished he'd get hungry again.

"Mind if I stay awhile?" he asked.

"We wouldn't even hear of your going!" said the rabbits. Then they plumped themselves down in the lion's lap and began to sing songs.

And somehow, even when it was time to say good night, that lion wasn't one bit hungry!

Home he went, through the soft moonlight, singing softly to himself. He curled up in his bed, patted his sleek, fat tummy, and smiled.

When he woke up in the morning, it was Monday.

"Time to chase monkeys!" said the lion.

But he wasn't one bit hungry for monkeys! What he wanted was some more of that tasty carrot stew. So off he went to visit the rabbits.

On Tuesday he didn't want kangaroos, and on Wednesday he didn't want zebras. He wasn't hungry for bears on Thursday, or camels on Friday, or elephants on Saturday.

All the big animals were so surprised and happy!

They dressed in their best and went to see the fat little rabbit.

"Rabbit," they said. "Oh, you wonderful rabbit! What in the world did you talk to the tawny, scrawny, hungry, terrible lion about?"

The fat little rabbit jumped up in the air and said, "Oh, my goodness! We had such a good time with that nice, jolly lion that I guess we forgot to talk about anything at all!"

And before the big animals could say one word, the tawny lion came skipping up the path. He had a basket of berries for the fat rabbit sisters, and a string of fish for the fat rabbit brothers, and a big bunch of daisies for the fat rabbit himself.

"I came for supper," he said, shaking paws all around.

Then he sat down in the soft grass, looking fat as butter, sleek as satin, and jolly as all get-out, all ready for another good big supper of carrot stew.

TITLE INDEX